I0771285

WTexas in *2* Plays:

LawnMaster and Winter Crew

by C. G. Wayne

Otter Track Press

MRose Group, LLC
Wetumpka, Al

Otter Track Press

Otter Track Press is a division of MRose Group, LLC. Wetumpka, Alabama. www.ottertrack.mrose.com

First Edition: January 2014

The characters portrayed in this narrative are fictitious. Any resemblance to actual persons living or dead is coincidental.

Wayne, Clifford Gordon.
        WTexas in 2 Plays / by C.G. Wayne—1st ed.

Summary: A narrative in dramatic form about the members of a grounds crew at a Texas university.

Library of Congress Control Number: 2014900093
ISBN: 978-0-9848229-2-8
[1. Fiction—Literature. 2. Post-modern—Fiction. 3. Plays—
Story Cycle]

Acknowledgements

*What I hope is that I have written a piece worthy of those
who have taught and worked with me.*

*The roots of this narrative cycle rest in a Stanford playwright
workshop conducted by Amy Freed many years ago. For me it
was a pivotal event. Thank you, Amy Freed, for being so kind
in your comments about my writing skills during the
workshop.*

*I've tried not to write for an audience
but to remain authentic to the experiences in my life.*

*I am grateful for the time and care expressed by the Others in
my life...*

wife and children

my Afghan Hounds, both here and departed

Montana, Markey, Jolie, Niki, and King Howl

my parents, grandparents,

*my friends including
Bill McAnulty, Lowell Lum, and Mike Smith who traded
stories with me for years about living in West Texas while we
sat on the other side of cubicle walls at work.*

*One person in particular I must mention from my young day is
Mr. Monroe who spent hours telling me of his cowboying life
in the early part of the 20th century working for a cattle
company near Ft. Worth. His life was worthy of a story of its
own and I was fortunate to know him. I always wish I had
listened closer so that I could recall every word.*

*As always, my hope is that this work doesn't embarrass them
while remaining true to the unique experiences of my existence
and those I've know whose voices were quickly lost to time.*

Front Cover: painting of a Tobiano colt near Marfa, TX. – by Jake (Theresa Wayne).

Back Cover: Chandhara's Rainbow Warrior (Howl) and Jendar's Body of Evidence (Niki) with the author and his wife at their house in Wetumpka, AL (8/2011). photo by Theresa Wayne.

Table of Contents

- W Texas in 2 Plays -

The title of this work is audacious. Saying something is "West Texas" covers a lot of diverse ground. Especially in the context of two plays. Typical big cultural generalizations of West Texas are oil and gas in Midland-Odessa, cattle in Abilene, and big agriculture in Lubbock. These are familiar representations in literature and film, usually depicted as the conflict of big oil displacing ranchers or the slide of a forgotten town fading into oblivion. But, to me, West Texas is more truthfully an abstract expression of the collective experience of people who inhabit the hard and beautiful wide open space west of Fort Worth. It is a collective and shared memory not a geographic locale.

This work is a vehicle intended to give voice to those whose lives are the embodiment of West Texas.

My understanding of West Texas comes from living on its edge, regularly traveling through its towns, listening to the stories of those who with their families had to leave it for better paying jobs in large cities, and hearing my grandmother's stories about my great-great grandfather's time ranching in 1880's West Texas. West Texas is a personal experience. Stories of the lights at Marfa, the tanks at Balmorhea, a small ranch at Toyahvale, and the temperate weather of the Davis Mountains were told with a persistent longing to return.

Once I worked with a man who told me of the time when he was a little boy and he and his dad drove their cattle down the brick streets of north Fort Worth into the stockyards. The days of driving cattle down the streets of Fort Worth as a routine part of everyday business are gone. But cattle drives, the White Elephant Saloon, and the cattle barons' homes on the bluff south of downtown (only a couple were left standing when I lived there) are echoes of the historical nexus that makes the culture of West Texas.

It is the experience of the land, weather, and hardship of Being in that place that is West Texas. When life is so necessarily focused on essentials, there is little room for trivia and pretense. Those things are left to the people who live in the east.

***

Last week, where I live now, the hard cold reminded me of the days in Fort Worth when weather was at its extreme. I lived in Fort Worth for more years than I had originally planned. It was a love-hate experience. Didn't care much for the heat in the summer or the hard cold of winter.

June to September of 1980 was hot. Really hot. 42 consecutive days over 100 degrees and three consecutive days of 113 degrees or more.

May was almost always a pleasant month and I was convinced back then that the pioneers crossing in their wagons must have reached the edge of the West Fork of the Trinity River in the spring, looked at the spread of Bluebonnets and Indian Paintbrush and decided that was good enough. July, August, and September might have changed their minds but by then they were settled in. That's what I thought at the time. But I stayed another seven years after that hot summer so I guess I was settled in myself.

Then there was December of 1983 when a mass of arctic air swept south, as far as Corpus Christi, froze the water in the bay there and killed the palms. Massive fish kill in the bay. In Fort Worth where we lived, ice formed on the inside glass of the windows and every one of my ligustrum in the backyard was killed. 14 degrees in Corpus, seems like it was 9 or 10 at the house in Fort Worth. But I stayed another four years after that cold winter.

Weather comes and goes, hot one year, cold the next, but enduring it and coming out ok and into the next season gave value to that hard time. I don't treasure the easy or careless as much as the things I complain about. The difficult is the thing that I value.

By 1987, I was living in Whittier, California telling stories about the heat and the cold in Texas. Living in California was easy compared to that but there was also no forgiveness in LA for screwing up. Maybe in a place where life is a hardscrabble to do better, there's more tolerance for trying and failing and trying again and again until you finally get it right.... if ever. Or, maybe I'm just nostalgic now about living on the edge of West Texas.

CGW

January 5, 2014

<u>*LawnMaster*</u>

LawnMaster

Characters

Mr. Hill also called LT	Early 50s. Grounds Dept Supervisor. Wears cowboy boots, jeans, shirt, and hat; clean, smoker, moderate drinker but not generally a bar room drinker, not a big talker.
Jake also called Gunny	Early 50s. Small engine mechanic. Unshaven weathered face, khaki work clothes, looks like a heavy drinker.
Francine	Late 20s/Early 30s. Runs the greenhouse. Wears no makeup, worn blue jeans and tank top, tan from outside hard work, a bit grubby, tough.
Eddy	Mid 30s. Grounds keeper. Part Cherokee Indian, smoker, moderate drinker, illiterate, wrinkled khaki work clothes, greasy, pomade hair, red face from too much sun, abrasive personality, missing teeth.
Perry	Mid to late 20s. Groundskeeper. Ladies' man, smoker, heavy bar room drinker, old blue jeans and polo shirt, flashy personality.
Steve (the Kid), and Richie	Early 20s. New employees. New jeans and denim shirts, squeaky clean, no smoking or drinking, very middle class and out of place.

Setting

One week in 1979. A Texas university grounds maintenance equipment workshop. Mr. Hill's office is on the right side. The door to the outside is on the left. In the center of the stage is a crate surrounded by four chairs and used as a table. At the back is a workbench with an old, grease stained coffee maker on it. Scattered around the area are leaf blowers, edgers, lawnmowers. The centerpiece of the equipment collection is a polished, gleaming riding mower, the LawnMaster.

Act 1

Scene 1

A rainy Monday morning in a grounds equipment workshop. The shop is dimly lit and filled with beat up and old equipment. Nothing in the shop is new or brightly painted. A cold front is blowing in out of the northwest. Francine, Perry, and Eddy sit in the center of the stage around a wooden crate that serves as a table. Jake is in the back, standing in front of a workbench, tightening bolts on engines and wiping down parts.

Mr. Hill, the supervisor, and Steve, a new employee, walk in from outside.

Mr. Hill	Ok, guys. Here's the new kid.
Steve	My name's Steve.
Mr. Hill	You. Eddy. I'm going to put him up at the tennis center with you and Brad.
Eddy	Ok.
Mr. Hill	After this rain lets up I want you and the kid to get those trees over by the pro shop trimmed. Eddy, you take the LawnMaster and the kid here can drive the Toro. Where's Brad?
Eddy	He's up at the tennis center.
Mr. Hill	What the hell is he doing up there?
Eddy	Don't know. Said something about planting flowers.
Mr. Hill	(_mutters_) Damn botanists.

Ok, kid. Over here's the time clock. Punch in when you get here and out when you leave. Be here at 7:30. We get started before the college kids wake up. Quitting time is 5. You get an hour for lunch and two paid 15 minute breaks during the day. Take 'em. I don't want any labor department trouble. Eddy, since Brad is hiding out up at the tennis center, show the Kid here the ropes.

Mr. Hill walks to his office and slams the door.

Eddy   Where you from, Kid?

Steve   Mississippi. My name's Steve.

Eddy   What the hell are you doing in Ft. Worth?

Steve   I was working at a lab. But I got laid off.

Eddy   What'd you do?

Steve   I was a chemist.

Eddy   Chemist?

Perry   No shit? Why you working on a grounds crew?

Steve   I'm going back to school. When you work full time for the school, they don't charge you tuition.

Eddy   Why you wanting to go to school? School never did me no good.

Perry   Hell, Eddy. You never even went to school.

Eddy   And I did pretty damn good without it.

Perry   All of us can see how good you done.

Eddy   Kid, you know anything about working on a grounds crew?

Steve   Not really.

Eddy   Shit.

Perry   You ever used one of these here mowers before?

Francine   Not likely. He's just a lawnboy.

They all laugh at the joke except for Steve.

Eddy   He didn't get it. I bet he's never even mowed a lawn. Look at them hands. Bet his folks have gardeners.

Perry   Hey, Kid. After this your old man can hire you and save himself some money. You guys want to play some cards?

Francine   Wait till Mr. Hill nods off.

Eddy   He's a mean one, Kid. Don't ever let him catch you screwin off on this job. Rides around in that white pickup of his just looking for guys screwin off. (*to the others*) Remember ol' Pete?

Perry   Hell yeah.

Eddy   Last year Hill caught him sleeping behind that building over there on the circle. Beat the living shit out of him.

Francine   That's a lie and you know it. Don't believe him, Kid. Besides, that was the third time Mr. Hill caught him sleeping over there.

Perry   Ol' Pete was wearing a cast on his hand after that.

Francine   Don't worry, Kid. Mr. Hill's just a old cowboy. Believes you do a days work for a days pay.

Perry   I ain't seen Pete since Laredo. Him and me was both in jail down there for a couple of days. Back in the winter. That Laredo was one hell of a jail. I was just in for being drunk, but ol' Pete'd hit a cop. They might of even sent him down to Henderson. I think they beat the shit out of him in jail too.

Eddy   Bastard never learned his lesson. Pete was stupid about things like that. Couldn't stop pushing. You know?

Perry   Shit. School wouldn't have helped him none either.

Perry pulls out a pack of cigarettes and lights one up.

Steve   You guys smoke in here?

Eddy   Sure. Why not?

Steve   All this gasoline and oil.

Perry   You know you can drop a lit cigarette in a tank of gas and nothing will happen. Thought you was a chemistry man.

Steve   What about the fumes?

Perry   Jake over yonder keeps the doors open so they don't collect.

Eddy   That Jake is another one you got to watch out for.

Perry   Yeah, he's real particular about how you take care of this crappy old equipment. Every time you go to take something out be sure to check the oil. If it needs oil, top it off. Otherwise, you throw a rod or cook a motor and Jake'll be all over your ass. He thinks all this here stuff is his.

Eddy   He's worse than Hill about these mowers.

Jake walks over to the group.

Jake   Goddamn right I am.

Perry   See, I told you he wasn't deaf.

Jake   Who said I was deaf?

Perry   Eddy did. He says so all the time.

Jake   Ain't true. I can still hear ok.

Eddy   Not me, Jake. I never said it. That was Perry.

Jake   Don't matter. You both been saying it since you got back here.

Perry   That's right, go ahead, be paranoid. What'cha going to do this fall, Kid?

Steve   Fall?

Eddy   When they let the groundskeepers go. This ain't permanent work you know. It's seasonal.

Steve   What do you do?

Perry   A bunch of us usually jump in my wagon and head down south. Grass still growing into fall down there.

Eddy   That's why spring's best. On weekends you get overtime doing campus work for them sports games they have.

Perry   College kids are always screwing something up.

Eddy   The overtime's good. But you got to rathole it for
               fall.

Perry   You ain't never ratholed anything Eddy. He's just big
               talk Kid, don't listen to him. He drinks every dime he
               gits.

Eddy   No, I don't. I got kids to take care of.

Eddy goes over to the LawnMaster and ignores them, starts wiping it down.

Perry   There he goes. Guess I made him mad.

Perry looks over at Mr. Hill's office.

               Hey guys, Hill's asleep.

Francine pulls out a deck of cards.

Francine   Usual?

Steve   What are you doing?

Perry   Playing BooRay, Kid. Want to play?

Steve   No. What's BooRay?

Francine   Fresh meat. He's never played BooRay.

She shuffles the cards. Jake sits on her right, between her and Perry.

LawnMaster

                    It's a card game they play back home.

Steve   I'll just watch.

Francine   Suit yourself. Hey, Eddy. You going to play or are
                    you still mad?

Eddy   I ain't mad. Just cleaning up my LawnMaster.

Perry   Eddy's in love with that mower. He polishes it every
                    night before we leave. You'd think it had tits or
                    something.

Francine   Hey, watch your mouth.

Perry   Sorry, Francine.

Francine   Eddy, ante up or clean your mower.

Eddy   Yes, Francine.

Perry   (*mocking Eddy*) Yes, Francine.

Francine   Shutup.

Eddy sits on Francine's left, between her and Perry.

Steve   How do you play this game?

Francine   It's like spades. Five players is best but we get by
                    with four. Brad doesn't know how to play so he

usually hides out at the tennis center. Before the deal, you got to ante up.

They all toss dollar bills into the center of the crate. Francine begins shuffling the cards.

We play a one buck ante. All antes go in the pot. What you want to do is win the pot by taking more tricks than anybody else. The other thing you want to do is burn anybody you can.

Perry   Francine's good at burning your ass.

Steve   What's that?

Perry   When you ante up, anybody that didn't take a trick has to match the new pot. That's burned. That's when you lose your ass.

Jake cuts the deck and Francine talks as she deals the cards.

Francine   The deal rotates clockwise every hand. The dealer shuffles and the person on the right cuts the deck. Then you deal out five cards going clockwise, one at a time and face down, with the dealer's last card face up.

Steve   Sounds complicated.

Francine   Not really. Watch.

Francine deals her last card face up and taps it with her finger.

	That's the trump suit for the round. A card of this suit always beats everything else. If you don't have a card of the suit that got lead, you can play a trump card to win the trick.

Jake   Hey. Let's play. LT's going to wake up before you get finished telling this kid how to play. I'm in.

Perry   I'm in. Besides, the Kid ain't playing anyway.

Eddy   Out.

Eddy puts his cards face down on the crate.

Francine   In. Once you get a look at your hand, you got to say if you're going to play the hand. If you go out, you lose your ante and put your cards face down on the crate like Eddy just did.

Jake puts three cards face down on the crate.

Jake   Give me three.

Francine gives him three cards.

Francine   Once you're in, you can replace any of your cards.

Perry puts two cards face down on the crate.

Perry   Two.

Francine gives him two cards.

Francine   Two.

She puts two down and picks up two from the deck.

                  Jake plays the first card. Everything in BooRay goes
                  counterclockwise from the dealer.

Jake   Com'on, Francine. Doggone it. No more table talk.
                  That's the rules. He's got to learn like the rest of us.

Eddy   Yeah. When you play, you play. We don't talk about
                  the deal, the cards, nothing. You want to talk about
                  the game? You go outside. Them's the rules.

Perry   Besides, the old man won't be sleeping long. Even
                  with the rain.

Francine   Ok, ok. Try to follow along, Kid.

Steve   My name is Steve.

*They play a fast hand, flipping the cards on the table. Perry takes the
pot. They all ante.*

Eddy   I thought you were going to burn old Jake there at the
                  end.

Jake   I'm too mean to get got.

*Eddy shuffles the cards and Francine cuts the deck. Eddy deals the
cards. Each one examines their hand.*

Francine   I'm in.

LawnMaster

Jake	Me too.

Perry	In.

Eddy   I'm in.

Francine   Gimme one.

Francine throws a card on the table and Eddy deals her another card.

Jake   Two.

Jake discards two and Eddy deals him two new cards.

Perry   One.

Perry discards one card. Jake stands up suddenly and steps between the crate and Hill's office.

Jake   He's moving.

They quickly clear the money off the crate and put the cards away. Jake walks back to his mowers.

Perry   I'm going outside to take a smoke. Want to go?

Eddy   Sure. I hate being cooped up in here.

Perry and Eddy walk outside.

Francine   Jake, I'm going over to the greenhouse.

Francine leaves. Steve walks over to Jake who is working on an engine.

Steve   Hi.

Jake looks up at him but says nothing and continues working. Steve watches him.

Jake   I'm busy, Kid.

Steve   My name's Steve. You've got a lot of mowers to keep up. How long've you been working here?

Jake   Since I got out of Henderson.

Steve   The prison?

Jake   Weren't no beauty school, Sherlock.

Steve   What'd you do?

Jake   Just take care of my equipment and we'll get along ok.

Steve   ok. How does that work?

Jake   What work?

Steve   Do we sign out the equipment somewhere?

Jake sighs and puts his tools down.

Jake   No. In the morning you come in here and LT tells you what he wants you to do that day. You get your gear, whatever you got to have, and go work.

Steve   Why do you call him LT?

Jake   'Cause I known him a long time. But he's Mr. Hill to you.

Steve   Ok. Where's the tennis center?

Jake   It's up the hill over there. We got a back road you take though. That way you don't bother any of them rich kids.

              Another thing… (*points at the mower*) …see that LawnMaster over there? Eddy thinks that's his. So don't mess with it. A month ago he was up there on that thing, mowing too close to the cars, and put some rocks into the front end of a Mercedes. LT was pissed over that. I expect that's why he's putting you up there. To be nice to them tennis people.

Steve   What's a groundskeeper do?

Jake   Dig ditches. Mow. Plant flowers. Whatever LT tells you to do.

Steve   Eddy was saying that he and Perry are seasonal

Jake   That's right. Me and Francine are permanent.

Jake motions to the equipment in the shop.

              I got all this to take care of. Francine gets the flowers and things ready for spring. That's her greenhouse back there.

Steve   Is she a horticulturist?

Jake   No. Francine's just a girl. From somewhere down in Louisiana I think. Why?

Steve   Just trying to get to know everybody.

Jake   I wouldn't. It's not worth the trouble.

Steve   Why not?

Jake   It just ain't. But knock yourself out if you want. In a month let me know what you think. After you get to know this crowd.

By the way. One more thing you ought to know about Eddy there, since you're going to be working with him and all. He can't read. Not a lick. And he gets real touchy about it. So don't let on you know he can't.

Steve   How does he get by?

Jake   He knows what the pictures mean on the labels. Look, I got to get this equipment ready for tomorrow.

Jake starts working on the equipment. Steve watches him.

You making me nervous, Kid. Why don't you go somewhere else for awhile.

LawnMaster

Steve   Is it ok to go see the greenhouse?

Jake   I ain't your momma.

Steve quietly walks away. Lights fade.

Scene 2

Midmorning on Monday, Jake is working alone in the workshop when Mr. Hill walks out of his office. Mr. Hill stands in the doorway watching Jake work.

Mr. Hill   What'cha think of this new kid, Gunny?

Jake   He won't stick. He asks too many questions. And he keeps tellin everybody his name.

Mr. Hill   Yeah, I noticed. Name seems kind of important to him, don't it?

Jake   He don't play cards neither.

Mr. Hill   Maybe he'll fit in with that bunch up at the tennis center.

Jake   Probably. But Eddy's going to give him hell.

Mr. Hill sits in a chair by the crate.

Mr. Hill   I ain't decided about that Eddy yet. He does ok but he's got a difficult streak in him.

Jake walks over and sits across from him.

Jake   This year he's actin' like that LawnMaster's his. Spends a lot of time polishing it.

Mr. Hill   That ain't good. What do you think he'd do if I let Perry use it to cut the grass over by the stadium?

Jake   Jeez. He might just up and quit.

Mr. Hill   Think so?

Jake   Maybe. He loves that mower.

Mr. Hill   Enough to quit?

Jake   That's Eddy. He's simple. Little things like that are
              about all he's got.

Mr. Hill   You win any money today?

Jake   Not today. Perry took the pot.

Mr. Hill   You'll get it back.

Jake   Maybe. Rain's almost stopped.

Mr. Hill   Yeah. I've been watching it. Looks like it'll be
              cleared out in an hour.

Jake   How're them dogs of yours doing?

Mr. Hill   Ok, I reckon. Sold one of my pointers to a dentist
              down in Houston last week. Fine dog. I'm going to
              miss that one.

Jake   Why'd you sell it, then?

Mr. Hill walks over to the door, looks out at the weather, takes a pack of cigarettes out of his shirt pocket, puts one in his mouth but doesn't light it.

Mr. Hill   It's just a dog.

Jake   Bull - Shit. I know you don't believe that.

Mr. Hill   I been thinking about this rain and I changed my mind about the work schedule this afternoon. Think I'll have a couple of 'em go clear gutters in the street over by the library.

Jake   Bet there's limbs down over by the admin building too.

Mr. Hill   Yeah. That old cottonwood always sheds a few. Even in a little rain like this. I'll send the rest of 'em over there. That should keep 'em out of trouble for the rest of the day.

Mr. Hill goes back into his office. In two beats, Francine and Steve walk in with Perry and Eddy behind them. Jake turns around, surprised.

Jake   What the hell.

Francine   Mr. Hill called us on the radios.

Jake   Wonders of the modern age. Nobody's safe anymore.

Mr. Hill steps out of his office.

LawnMaster

Mr. Hill   Heavy rain's going to be ending in a few minutes.
Francine, I want you and Perry to take one of the
Toro's up to the admin building and see if they got
any limbs that've come down. You get something to
haul back then radio me and I'll get a truck up to you.
Go on. Ya'll get going.

Francine and Perry pick up some keys and equipment from Jake.

Eddy, I want you to take the kid here up to the library
and make sure all them gutters in the streets up there
are clean. You know the grates that plug up first so
get 'em now. Grab some rakes and shovels and take
the old Toro. Give that botanist, Brad, a call. He's
been sitting on his ass long enough up there at that
tennis center.

Hell, second thought, I'll call him myself. Get on up
there. He'll met you. Radio if you need a truck to
haul any limbs. Don't use the old Toro for that.
They're too big.

*Eddy and Steve pick up some keys and equipment from Jake and all of
them leave. Hill waits for them to leave.*

I'm going to have Perry use that LawnMaster over at
the stadium tomorrow.

Jake   LT, why you want to do that? Eddy's going to get all
pissy.

Mr. Hill   That's the point. He's a grounds keeper. I ain't going to have any groundskeeper try to run my squad.

Jake   He's going to be out of here in a few more months. Hell, he may not even be back next year.

Mr. Hill   Sure he will. And most of the others too. I don't have budget to keep any goddamn prima donna groundskeepers.

Jake   You're the boss.

Mr. Hill   You goddamn right. And I'm going to put a end to this now, 'fore somebody else falls in love with any more of my equipment.

Mr. Hill walks to the door and stands there, looking outside.

That Brad is another one.

Jake   What's that?

Mr. Hill   I said that damn Brad was a prima donna too.

Jake   How'd you get one of them botanist to work for cheap, anyway?

Mr. Hill   He needed the work.

It's hard times. Folks don't need botanists when they ain't got fancy gardens. Worked out fine for me.

Jake   Shut up that tennis pro didn't it?

Mr. Hill   That woman was pissed when Eddy put those rocks into her car. Cost the school some money to fix that thing. Over 6 grand. I had to do something.

Jake   Damn. That was one of those expensive ones.

Mr. Hill   All them cars up there are. There ain't a one up there I could afford to drive. I told that bastard not to mow up there when they were having their lessons. I was that close… (*puts up two fingers squeezed tight together*) …to putting a lightening bolt up his ass over that one.

Mr. Hill sits down.

Jake   Eddy's a hardheaded sumbitch ain't he?

Mr. Hill   That's why I hired that Brad. Most places, Eddy screws up and nobody notices. But up there they got too much money for Eddy.

Jake   He don't like 'em neither.

Mr. Hill   No, he don't. He's got a real problem there.

Jake   Why don't you just put Perry up there? Make Eddy work out by the stadium?

Mr. Hill   That's one of those damned if you do, damned if you don't situations. Perry would be boosting the cars.

Jake   I don't know. I think he's smart enough to know he'd get caught if he was doing it up there. It ain't like being down at the mall.

Mr. Hill   Anyway. I don't want him up there. If it wasn't the cars, he'd be messing with those women.

Mr. Hill sips from his coffee mug.

                That'd be worse than Eddy puttin rocks through their windshields. My idea was that between Brad and this new kid, I could keep Eddy away from there most of the time.

Jake   Sounds like a plan.

Mr. Hill   Heard from any of the fellas lately?

Jake   Slim Jim called last week. He's up in Amarillo now, working on a oil well.

Mr. Hill   Good money. But I never took to that roustabout work.

Jake   Never tried it myself.

Mr. Hill   I didn't stick with it long. I missed working cattle too much. How long's Slim Jim been up there?

Jake   About a year now. Got himself a girlfriend and everything.

LawnMaster

Mr. Hill   Whoa. Now I'm surprised. That was one ugly sum-
                  bitch.

Jake   I bet she ain't much to look at either.

Mr. Hill   Never know about women. Sometimes they got
                  funny tastes in men.

Jake   Yeah. Yeah.

Mr. Hill   You ever hear from your wife?

Jake   Which one?

Mr. Hill   Any of 'em.

Jake   Hell no. They don't want no part of me.

Mr. Hill   What about your boy?

Jake   He went in the Air Force a year or so back and I ain't
                  heard from him since. But I reckon he's ok. Least I
                  ain't seen him on the news, thank god.

Mr. Hill   That's good. About all you could hope for, I guess.

Jake   Yeah. Didn't want no part of the Corps. (*Stares out
                  the door*) Looks like that rain's just about over.

Mr. Hill   Smells good don't it.

Jake

I can't smell nothing anymore. Gasoline fumes killed my sense of smell. Screwed up my sense of taste too. Never know how much losing one thing can change your life.

You ever think about getting married?

Mr. Hill

Me? Hell no. I got too old for that.

Jake

Age ain't got nothing to do with it. What if you walked in the Yellow Rose one night and see some fine lookin' woman sitting at the bar. Say, you buy her a drink, and then it just hits you.

Mr. Hill

Not likely. Don't think I'd spend any money on a woman at the Yellow Rose.

Jake

I would.

Mr. Hill

I know you would, that's why you been married so many times. But you ought to be saving that up for retirement, like me. What little bit of pension you got coming won't even pay your bar tab much less take care of no woman.

Jake

I ain't' retiring. I'm workin' 'til I drop over dead.

Mr. Hill

That's a ambition.

Jake

Hell, it's a plan.

LawnMaster

Mr. Hill   Plan, then.

Jake   How much longer you going to stick with this place,
                 here?

Mr. Hill   I don't have any set idea about that. I got to get
                 enough cash money put aside first.

Jake   That was always my problem back when I was mar-
                 ried.

Mr. Hill   Good reason not to get hooked up with a woman.

Jake   Well, maybe. It didn't help me none, that's for damn
                 sure. That last one was a high maintenance woman.
                 But a looker. Until we'd been married a few years.
                 Then she just sort of went down hill. Didn't take long
                 either. After I got put in Henderson though she
                 trimmed out real nice and she looks purty good now,
                 last time I saw her.

Mr. Hill   What you mean by "high maintenance"?

Jake   She liked expensive shit. You know how much those
                 Coach handbags cost?

Mr. Hill   Don't have a clue.

Jake   A bunch. She had some that cost almost three
                 hundred each. And she had to have 'em so they
                 matched the color of the shoes she was wearing.

Yeah, that's high maintenance. Sorry I brought it up. What a crazy life. Just crazy. Lost my shop keeping up with that.

Mr. Hill   Yeah, well, I'm going to go get some more smokes. You need anything from the QuickStop?

Jake   A couple packs of Picayunes.

Mr. Hill   Ok. Be back in about an hour.

Jake   Hour?

Mr. Hill   Yeah. I got to check on that Brad. He didn't want to go clean out gutters.

Jake   Sounds like he's becoming a pain in the ass.

Mr. Hill shakes his head as he leaves. Lights fade to black.

Scene 3

Monday afternoon in the equipment shop. Jake is alone in the shop working on equipment. Perry and Francine can be heard arguing.

Perry   I told you that wasn't going to work.

Francine   If you had helped me it would have.

Perry   I was. You just weren't paying any attention.

Francine   I never seen anybody so afraid of a grass snake before.

Perry   I couldn't see what kind it was. Hell, it might of been a moccasin.

Francine   We ain't got no moccasins up here. I keep telling you that. Rattlers. But no moccasins. This here is prairie land, not swamp.

Perry   Hell. That don't mean nothing. All the time you read about people putting piranhas out in lakes and shit. You never know.

Perry and Francine walk into the shop and hang their rain gear in the corner.

Francine   That's people with aquariums. Nobody keeps moccasins.

Perry   Never know. Maybe somebody did and then decided
                 to let it go in Lake Worth. Just like those iguanas
                 they got running wild in Los Angeles.

Francine   They ain't got no iguanas running wild in Los
                 Angeles.

Perry   Yeah they do. I saw it on the news. Big ones and
                 they're mean.

Francine   News? What kind of news?

They sit down facing each other.

Perry   You think you're so smart. One of these days you're
                 going to reach out to pick up one of them snakes and
                 its going to bite you. You're going to be real pissed
                 when it turns out I was right and somebody set some
                 moccasins loose.

Francine   You been out in the sun too long.

Jake   What're you two yakking about over there.

Francine   Perry's afraid of snakes.

Perry   No, I'm not. Just the poison ones. Hell, she don't
                 even look to see what kind it is. And then wants to
                 put it in the back of the Toro to drive it over to the
                 creek.

LawnMaster

Jake   Best to leave the snakes be, Francine.

Francine   It was just a coachwhip. He got up there by the oak
                        over at the library.

Jake   Hell, Perry. You afraid of a coachwhip?

Perry   I thought it was a moccasin. It was dark like one.

Francine   Moccasins are gray. You ever see a moccasin before?

Perry   Not exactly.

Jake   I don't reckon he has. Not many of them in Marfa is
                        it.

Perry   Tell her about the iguanas in Los Angeles.

Jake   What guanas?

Perry   Last week when we were in the Yellow Rose they
                        had it on the tv. Remember? The news article. And it
                        said how these iguanas would get so big that people
                        was letting them loose cause they'd get mean if you
                        didn't handle them all the time. And now they got
                        these big lizards all over the place out there.

Jake   Could be. I don't pay much attention to that tv when
                        I'm drinking.

Francine gets up and hands Jake the keys to the Toro and then sits down by the crate. Jake puts then in a drawer and goes back to working on the engines.

Perry   You ever been to Los Angeles?

Francine   No. You?

Perry   Every now and then. I go out there sometimes for a friend.

Francine   So, you ever seen any guanas out there?

Perry   I ain't exactly up in Hollywood when I'm out there.

Eddy and Steve's voices are shouting from outside the shop.

Eddy   Hey! Put the Toro over there.

Steve   Over here?

Perry   Sounds like they're a happy couple.

Eddy   No, you dumb shit. Over there. By the shed where the other one is.

Francine   Eddy's in a mood.

Eddy   And bring them tools in. You got to clean 'em so they don't rust.

Eddy walks into the shop carrying his rain gear, throws it in the corner, and sits down.

LawnMaster

Eddy   Damn. I hate cleaning those goddamn gutters.

Francine   You didn't hang your gear up.

Eddy   Bite me.

Francine   (*she glares at Eddy*) You wouldn't like it.

Eddy gets up, hangs his rain gear in the corner.

                        Did you dump the leaves over in my compost pile?

Eddy   Three loads of it. Mostly leaves and branches.

Perry   What branches?

Eddy sits down hard in the chair.

Eddy   We had a oak that lost a limb up there. Hell of a
                        mess.

Francine   Did you call Mr. Hill?

Eddy   For what?

Francine   You idiot. You're supposed to call Mr. Hill when
                        stuff like that happens.

Eddy   I took care of it.

Francine   He wants the truck to haul them limbs, not the old
                        Toro.

Eddy   It wasn't a big limb.

Perry   You're such an ass. It can't haul that kind of load.

Francine   If it come off the oak up there it was big.

Steve walks in, hangs his gear in the corner.

                Hey, Kid. Was that a big limb you guys hauled?

Steve   Sure, but I rode in the back and held it on.

Francine   (*she glares at Eddy*) Busted. Mr. Hill's going to be pissed.

Eddy   I don't give a shit.

Eddy hunches his shoulders.

                We got it done. That's what counts.

Francine   No, it doesn't. You burn up that Toro it doesn't count at all.

Eddy gets up and stalks out to smoke.

Steve   What's wrong?

Perry   You guys have to call Mr. Hill if you haul more than leaves and trash.

Francine   The old Toro's only for light hauling.

LawnMaster

She shouts over to Jake.

Jake. Eddy hauled back a bunch of big limbs with
that old Toro.

Jake   What?

Francine   Eddy hauled a bunch of heavy limbs in the old Toro.

Jake   Hell's bells. Tell him to bring it in. I'll have to check
                  it first thing in the morning.

Francine   I'll run him down. He already took off.

Francine leaves the shop to find Eddy.

Jake   LT's goin to be pissed.

Perry   So, Kid, how was your first day on the ground crew?

Steve   I've had better days. Where do you clean off the
                  tools?

Perry   Usually, you wash 'em off outside first. Then over
                  there by Jake's some rags you can use. And some oil.
                  Wipe 'em down with the oil after you clean 'em. You
                  got any dirt stuck on 'em?

Steve   No.

He shows Perry the shovel and rakes.

Perry   Don't wash 'em then. Just wipe 'em down. Better
               hurry it up. Only a couple of minutes before we clock
               out.

*Steve takes a rag from Jake and starts wiping down the tools. Outside
of the shop, Francine and Eddy shout at each other.*

Francine   Hey, Eddy. Jake says to bring the old Toro in. He has
               to check it out tomorrow.

Eddy   Tell him I got to run back up the hill and get my
               gloves. I'll put it inside when I get back.

Francine enters the shop and goes over to Jake.

Francine   Eddy left his gloves. He said he'd bring it in when he
               gets back.

Jake   Hope it ain't long, I'm all set to go.

Francine   You going over to the Yellow Rose again?

Jake   Yeah, happy hour. Want to go?

Francine   No. Not me. Why you go over there every night?

Jake   They got a good happy hour.

Francine   Well, that's a routine.

Jake   Sometimes routine's ok. Beats the hell out of eating
               alone.

LawnMaster

Perry   Time to hit the clock!

Francine   Bye.

Jake   Yeah. See yah.

Francine   You be good tonight.

Jake walks over to the door and stands, looking outside.

Jake   Where's that goddamn Eddy?

Mr. Hill walks in.

Mr. Hill   What are you still doing here?

Jake   Waiting on Eddy. He had to go back and get his
                 gloves.

Mr. Hill   So.

Jake   He's got the Toro. He'll be in, in a couple of minutes.

Mr. Hill   You going over to the Yellow Rose?

Jake   Is the Pope Catholic?

Mr. Hill   I ain't decided yet.

Jake   What about you. You going over?

Mr. Hill   Not tonight.

Jake   What'cha doing?

Mr. Hill   Nothing particular. I was just thinking I'd go home early.

Jake   You getting old on me?

Mr. Hill   Hell, I been old. You too.

Jake   Not me. What's the forecast tomorrow?

Mr. Hill   More rain in the morning but clear by 10 or so.

Jake   No mowing then.

Mr. Hill   Too wet. I'm going to have 'em catch up on trim work.

Jake   Do you ever get tired of this yardman stuff?

Mr. Hill   I don't think about it.

Jake   I do. All the things we done when we was young. And here we are.

Mr. Hill   You tired of it?

Jake   Hell yes. Some days more than others.

Mr. Hill   What else would you do?

Jake   I don't know anymore.

LawnMaster

Mr. Hill	Me either. Tomorrow's just another day.

Jake   I'll have them weedeaters and leaf blowers ready.

Mr. Hill   Sounds like a winner. How long you going to wait around for that clown.

Jake   Till he gets here. I got to lock up the keys for I leave.

Mr. Hill   Ok then. I'm headin out. Lock 'er up when you leave.

Jake   You got it.

Mr. Hill leaves Jake standing by the door, talking to no one but air.

Where the hell did you leave them gloves. My beer's getting warm. There he is. (*Shouting*) Just leave it out there. I'll bring it in tomorrow. When I'm ready.

Eddy walks in and hands Jake the keys.

'Bout time. Where in hell did you leave them things. Mexico?

Eddy   No. They was up by the liberry.

Jake   You going over to the Rose?

Eddy   I don't think so. I ain't got any money this week.

Jake   Hell, you were playing cards today!

Eddy   That's all I had.

Jake   Damn. If you didn't have any money why were you
                playing cards?

Eddy   I might have won.

Jake   I don't know about you, Eddy. Tell you what. I'll buy
                a pitcher and split it with you.

Eddy   Thanks.

Jake   Com'on, let's get. You can give me a ride over there.

*They walk to the door. Jake flips the lights off and they leave the shop.
Jake closes the door behind them.*

- LawnMaster -

Act 2

Scene 1

Early Tuesday morning in the equipment shop. The shop is dark and empty. Jake can be heard talking outside.

Jake   Man, I got to stop drinking so much.

He flips the lights on in the shop.

Morning babies, time to rise and shine. Someday I'm going to work somewhere they got coffee made and waiting for me when I walk in.

Jake walks over to the coffee maker and pulls down a can of pre-ground, commercial coffee, and starts fixing a pot of coffee.

And some of that expensive coffee like they got at those shops in the mall.

He pours the water into the coffee maker.

And some of that special bottled water. Never get any of that in here. Hell we're doing good to get tap water.

He pushes the switch and watches to be sure it's dripping.

Nuther day in paradise.

Mr. Hill walks into the shop.

LawnMaster

Mr. Hill   Coffee ready yet?

Jake   It's working at it. Another couple of minutes.

Mr. Hill   You go over to that bar last night?

Jake   You bet.

Mr. Hill   I don't see how you do it. Don't think I could get up
                mornings if I did that every night.

Jake   I don't get drunk every night. I just go in and
                socialize a little 'for I get back to my trailer.

Mr. Hill   You need to get some dogs, or something you have to
                go home and take care of.

Jake   That's why I ain't got none. Don't care much for
                keeping animals.

                Had a horse once, though.

Mr. Hill   When was that? I don't remember you ever saying
                anything about having a horse.

Jake   It was right after I got out of the Corps. When I got
                out I went on back there to Tin Top.

                I was staying in the old bunk house on my folks'
                place out there.

Mr. Hill   What kind of horse?

Jake   A paint.

Mr. Hill   That's a good one. Where'd you get it?

Jake   Here. Right here in Ft. Worth at the Fat Stock show.
                Me and dad were over showing some stock. He had
                this bull he was real proud of, a Gertrudis. That was a
                big ol' bull.

                Ol' dad, you know, he started out on the King Ranch,
                so he always had them Gertrudis.

Mr. Hill   That King Ranch is a big spread.

Jake   It's not the same anymore. Not like back in his day.

Mr. Hill   Nothing ever is. So what happened to your horse?

Jake   Well, I was in town with dad at the stock show a few
                years later. That's when I met this girl one night and
                we run off and got married. That one was Shirley.

                I never went back to Tin Top after that. Ol' dad had
                that horse till they got killed.

Mr. Hill   You ain't never told me anything about that neither.

Jake   No. I ain't.

Mr. Hill   What happened to 'em?

Jake Well, they was out riding fence one spring and got caught down in a ravine by a flash flood. You know how it is in the spring. Happened too quick for him and Zulu to get up out of there. Zulu was what I named my horse. For Zulu Time. He was just a colt when I got him.

Anyway, they found him and Zulu about a quarter mile down from where they went in. They was all wrapped up in fence wire.

Mr. Hill That's ranching, ain't it? Work like hell all your life. Then get caught out down in a ravine one day.

Jake It's a bitch. Coffee's up.

Jake picks up the coffee pot and pours Mr. Hill and himself a cup.

When the hell are you going to buy me a decent coffee maker.

Mr. Hill No budget for it.

Jake Hell, LT. Look at this thing.

He motions at the machine in disgust.

The little red light's burned out on it now. Some mornings I stand around waiting on the damn thing to brew before I realize the switch ain't even caught.

Mr. Hill You been keeping it working.

Jake   Maybe I ought to stop patching this old thing then.

Mr. Hill   Wouldn't be no more coffee in the mornings if you did.

Jake   When'd you get so tight for money?

Mr. Hill   Since there ain't none. That's when. You'll just have to tough it out a little longer. Damn, Gunny, I remember seeing you make that stuff in your mess kit. You don't need any fancy coffee maker.

Jake   I ain't 20 no more. I want one of them automatic ones. The kind that automatically grinds the beans and brews it for you. That way I can just walk in and smell fresh brew in the mornings.

Mr. Hill   My budget got hit having to add that Brad to the payroll.

Jake   Thought you said he was cheap.

Mr. Hill   For a botanist. Not for this place.

Jake   What'cha going to do when you give up this yardman life?

Mr. Hill   I got me that house over in White Settlement. I aim to have it paid for. And probably keep me a few bird dogs.

Jake   Hell, that ain't no different from what you're doing now. Why don't you do something different?

Mr. Hill   Like what?

Jake   Get yourself one of them motorhomes and drive up to Alaska.

Mr. Hill   Too cold.

Jake   Not in the summer.

Mr. Hill   Ain't anything in Alaska I got to see.

Jake   All right then what about going to see some of those old battle fields you used to talk about.

Mr. Hill   We'll see. I got time to decide.

He sips his coffee.

                They're going to start drifting in before long.

Jake   Francine is usually first in.

Mr. Hill   She's a good one.

Jake   Seems to be pretty steady. She loves that greenhouse.

Mr. Hill   Between you and me, I'd like for you to keep a eye on Perry. Seems like he spends more'n his share of time getting drunk and waking up in jail.

Jake   He ain't no worse than any of us was when we were
                his age.

Mr. Hill   I ain't ever been in jail.

Jake   Except that time in Tokyo.

Mr. Hill   Except for that time. I forgot about that. That was a
                long time back.

Jake   I'll keep an eye on him.

Mr. Hill   Good. You were always a good lead man.

                I think the rain is going to hit about 8 so lets hold 'em
                here a few minutes to see what happens.

Jake   You got it.

*Mr. Hill goes into his office and Jake walks over to the door with his
cup of coffee to wait for the others to arrive.*

                (*shouts*) Coffee's on.

Francine's voice comes from outside of the shop.

Francine   Good lord. How do you manage to look so awake this
                early in the morning?

Jake   Nobody said I been to sleep yet.

Francine   You weren't out all night were you?

LawnMaster

Jake   It was a wild time. You should have been there.

Francine   No thanks. I like my life plain.

Jake   You're a find, you are.

Francine walks in the door.

Francine   Where's that coffee?

She walks over to the coffee pot, picks up her mug, and pours a cup.

                  You really weren't out all night were you?

Jake   No. Not me. I was home before the late news.

Francine   Good. What's on our schedule today?

Jake   LT wants everybody to stick around the shop for a
                  few minutes so he can see what the weather is going
                  to do.

Francine   I think it's going to rain.

Jake   Could be.

Perry walks in.

Perry   Hey you mugs.

Francine   Hey yourself.

50

Jake   Get yourself some coffee. LT wants you to wait around till he can decide what the weather's going to do.

Perry   Great. Maybe I can win some more money.

Perry walks over to the coffee maker, picks up his mug, and pours himself a cup.

Francine   Don't hold your breath, it's just going to be a light rain. You might as well start thinking about that sprinkler line you got to repair. You're going to be digging in the mud today, boy.

Perry   I ain't no boy.

Steve walks in. Francine walks over to a chair by the crate and sits down.

Francine   Hey, Kid.

Perry   Decided to come back for another day?

Steve   What are we doing today?

Francine   Waiting. Mr. Hill's getting the weather report.

Eddy walks in. Perry sits in the chair opposite from Francine.

Eddy   Jake, I don't see how you do it.

Francine   Do what?

LawnMaster

| Eddy | I went with him over to the Rose last night. Damn that man can drink. And look at him over there. Jake, what time did you get in here? |

Jake   Usual time. Why?

Eddy   How do you wake up in the mornings?

Jake   Practice, Eddy. Practice. I must of done it just about
            ever' day of my life. So far.

Eddy walks over to the coffee pot, picks up his mug, and pours a cup of coffee.

Perry   I didn't know you guys were going over there.

Jake   I go over there most every night.

Francine   You got no business going over there, Perry.

Perry   They got a dart league.

Eddy sits by the crate.

Francine   Drunks and darts. Now that's got to be exciting.

Perry   When I was down in Houston, I used to go over to
            this bar down in Clearlake where the astronauts hang
            out. It was really cool. They had a dart league.

Jake   I never learned darts.

Francine   Me neither. Always made me nervous.

52

| Steve | Is it ok if I get some coffee? |

| Francine | Sure, Kid. Did you bring a cup or something? |

| Steve | No. I didn't think about it. |

| Francine | Jake, you got an old cup the kid can use? |

| Jake | Maybe. |

Jake rummages through his stuff, pulls out a mug holding spare parts, and dumps it out on his desk.

Here, Kid. You can use this one. Might want to wash it out first.

| Steve | Where's a sink? |

| Jake | Bathroom. Over there. |

Steve leaves to clean out the mug.

| Francine | Were you any good at darts? |

| Perry | I was ok. I got on a team. |

| Jake | I ain't never seen any darts at the Rose. |

| Perry | You never noticed that wood box they got up on the wall down at the end of the bar? |

| Jake | Nope. Never noticed. What's it look like. |

Perry   A wood box.

Jake   Smartass. I thought they used a target of some kind.

Perry   It's all inside the box, Jake. Damn.

Jake   Don't get your panties in a twist. Shit. Sorry,
                    Francine.

Francine   You guys.

Jake   I said I was sorry.

                    (*to Perry*) See what you made me do.

Perry laughs.

Perry   You said that all by yourself.

Steve pours his coffee and stands outside the group, watching them.

Jake   Anyway, I never noticed any wood box on the wall at
                    the Rose.

Jake goes back to his work area.

Eddy   Why are we waiting around here?

Francine   Mr. Hill wants us to hold up till he knows what the
                    weather is going to do.

Eddy   Hell, I can tell you what the weather is going to do. I don't have to watch no radar on tv to know it's going to fair off.

Francine   And how do you know that?

Eddy   Look at the sky (*pointing to the door*). It's thinning out over there.

Francine   That doesn't mean anything. The weather's moving in from the northwest. That's east.

Eddy   No, it's not. (*points to Mr. Hill's office*) East is over there.

Perry   Hey, Eddy. What side of your house does the sun come up on in the morning?

Eddy   (*points to the door*) That side.

Perry   (*sarcastically*) You know Francine. I think he's right. Looks like he's got you this time.

Francine   Yeah, right.

Eddy   Hey, Kid. When Hill tells us we can get up to the tennis center you need to haul the tools up in the Toro. I got the LawnMaster and there ain't no place on it to haul tools.

LawnMaster

Francine   Jake, did you finish checking out that old Toro Eddy
                  burned up yesterday?

Jake   Shit. I forgot all about it.

Steve   Do you want me to bring it in?

Jake   No. I'll check it outside. Don't want it getting my
                  floor muddy.

Jake pulls out a key and picks up a handful of tools.

Eddy   You're just wasting your time. Ain't nothing wrong
                  with it.

Jake   Guess that's why I'm the one responsible for all this
                  here equipment and you're just a temporary
                  groundskeeper.

Perry   That hurt, Jake.

Jake   You break my equipment, we can't replace it. But LT
                  can always find another you to push a mower. Don't
                  forget it.

*They stand around quietly for a beat while Jake goes outside to work
on the Toro.*

Eddy   That's what's wrong with this place. They don't
                  know what it takes to get a job done. So busy
                  catering to these damn college kids. The priorities
                  around here are all screwed up.

Francine   You say the stupidest things. What kind of moron are
               you anyway?

Eddy   I ain't no moron.

Francine   You don't know what moron means, do you?

Eddy   You're in a bitchy mood.

Perry   Ok. That's not helping things. How about we talk
               about what we watched on tv last night? I got this
               descrambler last week from a guy I know and I can
               get all the channels. You all want one? I could sell
               you one for 25 dollars. You'd save that much the first
               month with this box.

Francine   You talking about one of those illegal descramblers?

Perry   No, no, no. It's not illegal. The signals are there on
               the cable. It's just a decoder box.

Francine   That ain't legal.

Perry   Jim said it was.

Francine   That's stupid. You're going to end up in jail, for real.

Eddy   Perry, how many times you been in jail?

Perry   About six I reckon.

LawnMaster

Francine   For what?

Perry   First was boosting a pickup truck when I was a kid.
                  That was just reform school though so it might not
                  count.

Francine   How old were you?

Perry   Twelve. I grew up down in Marfa. Nothing much else
                  to do down there except raise hell on the weekends.

Eddy   Never been there.

Francine   I heard of it. That's where they got those lights.

Perry   Yeah, they're weird. Anyway the truck was over at a
                  bar out on the edge of town. The guy was one of
                  those ranchers in town for something to drink… (*he
                  glances at Francine*) …and stuff. So I hot wired his
                  truck and drove on up to Fort Davis. They caught me
                  up there.

Francine   What'd your momma say.

Perry   Nothing.

Francine   You an only child?

Perry   Yeah. (*he stands up and looks out the door*) Hey,
                  looks like it's raining.

Eddy   Shit.

Francine   No mowing today. Better get the rain gear.

Jake runs in.

Jake   Rain almost got me. The old Toro's set. Don't haul any more big limbs in it. You'll take out the transmission next time. Hear me?

Eddy   Lousy piece of equipment if you can't use it.

Jake   I keep telling you, it ain't supposed to haul heavy limbs and shit. It never was. It's only supposed to be hauling your ass and some tools.

Eddy   Ok, ok. I heard you.

Jake   You do it again and I'll get LT to fire your ass.

Mr. Hill walks out of his office. Everybody stands up and moves out from around the crate.

Mr. Hill   What's that, Gunny?

Jake   Nothing, yet. Just talking about the equipment is all.

Mr. Hill   Looks like we got a little bit of light rain this morning. (*he looks around the room*) I see the botanist didn't make it down here again.

Jake   We ain't seen him for a few days now.

LawnMaster

Mr. Hill	Ok. I'll take care of that. Today, I want you guys to go ahead and get started. It's just going to be a light rain. No sitting around here on your butts like yesterday.
Francine	What about that sprinkler leak?
Mr. Hill	Right. Perry, take care of it on your way over to the admin building. It ain't much of a leak. Perry, take the Kid with you and show him how to repair a sprinkler leak.
Eddy	Hey, I thought he was going to work for me.
Mr. Hill	He works for me, just like you. As for you, you're going back up at the library to clean those gutters out.
Eddy	Damn.
Mr. Hill	What's that?
Eddy	Nothing.
Mr. Hill	That's right.

He turns back to the others.

Francine, I want you to spend today getting the annuals ready to plant. Tomorrow I think we need to get those put out. If we wait any longer the hot weather'll catch us.

Ok, everybody. You know the drill. Get your gear and go do some work. I've got to go talk to our professional up at the tennis center.

They all get their keys and rain gear.

Francine   How long do you think this rain is going to last?

Mr. Hill   About 2 hours. But it'll be light. Nothing hard like yesterday.

Perry   That's good. These Toro's ain't got no doors on 'em you know.

Mr. Hill   I know. But you won't melt. Ok, get going. I don't want any flooding out in the streets.

They begin to walk out the door.

Hey, you see any lightening, get out from under those trees. I lost a man once from that. Don't want that again.

Eddy   Hell. I'll be glad when this rain ends.

Mr. Hill   Eddy, if you run out of work to do up there by the library then go on down to the ag center. You can clean up down there.

LawnMaster

They all leave wearing rain gear. Mr. Hill stands in the door, coffee cup and cigarette in his hands, watching them.

Mr. Hill   What a squad.

Jake   You hired 'em.

Mr. Hill   Yes, I did, didn't I.

Jake   Changed your mind about Eddy?

Mr. Hill   I ain't sure yet. He bothers me.

Jake   Don't seem to be too predictable.

Mr. Hill   What was the deal about the equipment.

Jake   What equipment?

Mr. Hill   Don't bullshit me, Gunny. What did he screw up this time?

Jake   Nothing. I was just riding him a bit about taking care of the old Toro.

Mr. Hill   He's not too keen on cleaning up trash is he.

Jake   Not much. But I don't blame him.

Mr. Hill   Got to be done.

Jake   I know. But it ain't much fun I reckon.

Mr. Hill   Not like blasting up and down the hill on that goddamn ridin' mower. I seen him out there going hell bent for leather on that thing. Damn, you can hear it whining a mile away.

Jake   It's that hydraulic drive they got. Sounds like a sewin machine.

Mr. Hill   I was thinking it sounded more like a jet engine.

Jake   There ain't no roar.

Mr. Hill   Not the exhaust. The turbine.

Jake   Maybe a turbine.

Mr. Hill   You ever been on a jet?

Jake   Once. When I went out to see my son.

Mr. Hill   Where was that?

Jake   California. Little place out from L.A. called Norco. God, that was one dry, dusty place.

Mr. Hill   I was out there for a bit when I was rodeoing. Not Norco, but some of them little towns out there. Palmdale. Victorville.

Jake   I never knew you did any rodeoing.

LawnMaster

Mr. Hill   It was right before I lost my ranch. I was trying most
                  anything to make a little extra money.

Jake   Damn. How'd you get into that?

Mr. Hill   Had a good cutting horse. That's how I got in it. But
                  the money was in bull riding so I gave that a try.

Jake   How long'd you do that?

Mr. Hill   Just long enough to break my leg. I was a desperate
                  man. Lost my ranch anyway. (*looks at his watch*) I
                  gotta get on up to the tennis center and have a little
                  talk with Brad. He ain't worked out.

Jake   That's a shame.

Mr. Hill   I hate to cut him loose, but not everybody's cut out
                  for it. Francine'll have to take over up there till I get
                  somebody to replace him.

Jake   That ain't gonna make Eddy very happy.

Mr. Hill   We're going to get to see what kind of character that
                  Eddy's got.

Jake   I wouldn't have your job if they paid me good
                  money.

Mr. Hill waves him off and walks outside. Lights fade to black.

Scene 2

Friday evening in the Yellow Rose. A small bar with a couple of small tables and chairs. Very dark. A light over the table where Jake, Perry, and Eddy are sitting with an almost empty pitcher of beer, their mugs, and a plate of small sausages. Waylon Jennings music is playing, Are You Sure Hank Done It This Way. In a back corner shadow, unseen by the three at the table sits Mr. Hill watching the three drink beer and eat.

Jake   You fellas do ok today?

Eddy   Man. I hate gardening.

Jake   Why'd you sign up for this job then?

Eddy   I can't be inside. I got to work outside.

Jake   You mean like clastrophobia?

Eddy   I just don't like being inside for long.

Perry   What do you do when you go home?

Eddy   Most of the time I just work outside till supper. I got to be out where I can move around.

Jake   You ever get beat when you was a chap?

Eddy   Not worse'n anybody else.

Jake   Ever get shut up in a room?

Perry   Let's talk about something else. You're giving me the creeps.

Jake   Sure. No problem.

Eddy   What can we talk about?

Jake   Anything. You do much fishing?

Eddy   Me?

Jake   Either one of you. This is just conversation.

Perry   No.

Jake   Yeah. I reckon they don't do much fishing down in Marfa.

Perry   Least ways I didn't. Some of them ranchers, they had boats and all and would go over to the coast or a lake on vacation. But we never did any of that.

Jake   What about you, Eddy? Ever go fishing?

Eddy   Some.

Jake   Where 'bouts are you from any way?

Eddy   Around. We moved around a lot when I was growing up.

Jake   Ever live any place but Texas?

Eddy   Oklahoma some. Mostly up by Tahlequah. My momma had some folks up that way.

Perry   I been up there once or twice.

Jake   Got some good people live out that way. Your momma Cherokee?

Eddy   Part Cherokee.

Jake   Where else you live?

Eddy   One time we went to Arkansas. Around Ft Smith.

Perry   Why'd ya'll move around so much?

Eddy   We worked crops.

Jake   Ever get out around Tin Top?

Eddy   Weatherford. But not Tin Top.

Perry   What's in Weatherford?

Eddy   Peaches. We was usually there for that.

Perry   You ever pick any crops or was it just your folks.

Eddy   We all picked. Bunch of us kids. There wadnt any room for somebody not working.

Jake   No. I guess there ain't.

LawnMaster

Jake pours out the last of the pitcher.

Want another pitcher?

Eddy   Sure, boss.

Jake   Don't ever call me boss. LT's the boss. I'm just Jake.

Perry   I thought you didn't drink beer.

Jake   I don't. But I don't drink alone neither.

Jake leaves the table to get another pitcher of beer. While he's gone Eddy and Perry eat all of the sausages.

Eddy   Why do you think he asked us to come over here with him?

Perry   I reckon he was looking for somebody to drink with. He said he don't like to drink alone.

Eddy   But, he comes over here every night.

Perry   So, what's that mean?

Eddy   He ain't never asked both of us to tag along before.

Perry   Just go with it, Eddy. Sometimes people do a thing to be nice. Maybe that's what it is.

Eddy   I don't think so. Jake don't make me think of some-body that does things for nice.

Perry	Then we'll have to see what it is he's getting at. In the meantime eat some more of them little sausages. They're purty good for bar food.

Jake arrives with a full pitcher of beer.

Jake	Here you go.

He pours a round.

	Damn. You guys ate all them little sausages.
Perry	Sorry, Jake.
Jake	Sorry they're gone's more like it.

Jake leaves to get more sausages.

Perry	How you like working for Francine?
Eddy	I ain't workin for Francine.
Perry	Who you think runs everything now that Brad got his butt fired?
Eddy	That ain't working for her.
Perry	She's going to have you trimming her roses for her.
Eddy	She ain't my boss.

Perry   You wait till she chews your ass for screwing up
               some of them roses of hers. She's real picky about
               how them things is trimmed.

Eddy   I ain't working for no woman.

Perry   The hell you say. I bet tomorrow she's got your ass
               over there in that compost pile turning that sumbitch.

Eddy   Mr. Hill said I was working up at the admin building.

Perry   Till she tells you to turn compost. Then you'll be out
               there with a fork turning that shit. And she's real
               picky about that to.

Eddy   I ain't doing it.

Perry   Dumbass, you just ain't figured it out yet, have you?

Eddy   Don't call me dumb.

Perry   I call it how I see it.

Eddy   Just cause I didn't get as much schooling…

Perry   …any schooling…

Eddy   …doesn't make me stupid. I work damn hard feedin
               my family.

Perry   You got to have more going for you than working
           hard. Don't you ever look around?

Eddy   Sure I look around. What are you talking about
           anyway. Look around? At what?

Perry   All them college kids. They ain't workin a lick at all
           and they got ten times what we got.

Eddy   That's 'cause they already rich.

Perry   Ten years from now you're going to be sitting here at
           this table drinking beer same as now. Working hard
           and all. Listening to those little shits talking about
           some business deal they got going, and you ain't
           never getting nowhere.

Eddy   With you sitting right here too.

Perry   But I ain't working hard.

Eddy   That's why you won't last. You just a boy playing all
           day.

Perry   Shit. I could work you into the ground, any day. And
           I ain't working for no woman.

Eddy   Me either.

Perry   You're Francine's boy now.

Eddy   Bullshit.

Perry   (*imitates Francine*) You ever trimmed roses before?

Eddy   Bastard.

Perry   (*stands up*) Call me that again and I'll cut your fuckin
                head off.

Eddy   (*stands up*) You aint got the balls.

Jake walks up with a plate of sausages and crackers.

Jake   What the hell! You two lost your goddamn minds?
                Sit down you two 'fore you get us throwed out of
                here!

Perry sits down.

                Sumbitch. I ask you two red necks over here to my
                bar and look what you done. Damn near get us
                throwed out.

Perry   Sorry, Jake.

Jake   You been saying that all night. I don't want to hear
                no more "sorry." That don't mean shit comin from
                you. Sit down Eddy. You look like a bantee rooster
                standing there. Damn it. When you got to work with
                somebody you make the most of it and get along.
                Unless you want to get along. LT can arrange that if
                you like.

Eddy   I ain't working for no woman. I don't care if it is Francine.

Jake   You ain't working for Francine. You work for LT.

Eddy   I ain't turning no compost with no fork.

Jake   What the hell are you talking about now?

Eddy   I got to go home.

Eddy leaves.

Jake   What the hell were you two going on about?

Perry   He called me a bastard.

Jake   Figure of speech, boy. That's all. Why'd he call you that? You been telling him he was working for Francine?

Perry   He's a freak. A real freakazoid.

Jake   Damn. That's why I had you two sumbitch's come over here tonight. We got to get this thing put to rest or it ain't gonna be no good this summer. I seen it before. Two like you can just rip the heart out of a squad with all your pissy little prancing about. And over nothing. Over nothing, damnit. Go on. Git. I had enough of both you.

LawnMaster

Perry gets up from the table and leaves. Jake sits at the table with the empty mugs and full pitcher while the outlaw cowboy music plays. Mr. Hill walks up carrying his hi-ball glass and sits down at the table with Jake.

Mr. Hill   Howdy Jake.

He picks up a sausage from the platter and eats it.

Jake   LT, what're you doing over here?

Mr. Hill   Saw you and the two young bulls heading off this

                  way. Just thought I'd check in on you.

Jake   Where you been?

He looks around the room trying to locate the empty chair.

Mr. Hill   Sitting back yonder (*he tilts his head in the direction

                  of the table*). You're a good man Jake.

Jake   No, I ain't. I'm just a old man.

Mr. Hill   Think we got a problem brewing?

Jake   I do. Like smelling rain coming.

Mr. Hill   That's a good smell.

Jake   No it ain't. It's a smell something's going to happen.

                  If you get a tornado it ain't a good smell.

Mr. Hill   I get your point.

Jake   Remember when we was in country and ol' Slim Jim was in a pissin contest with that corporal?

Mr. Hill I remember.

Jake   Well, this is like that. And I don't know why you keep pushing Eddy like you are.

Mr. Hill Just trying to limber him up.

Jake   Well, he ain't limber.

Mr. Hill No, he ain't.

Jake   So why you pushing him?

Mr. Hill I can't stand seeing somebody with such piss poor character he got to have a special lawn mower to feel important.

Jake   Maybe he ain't got much more going for him than that.

Mr. Hill Then he ain't much of a man. I see 'em all the time. Specially around here. Lawn mower, car, house, it's all the same. Same weakness, different scale.

Jake   Damn LT. Why get all wrapped around the axle over this guy? He ain't nobody special.

Mr. Hill	I hired him. He works for me. Boy needs to get a bigger view of life.
Jake	That don't make sense, LT. How's he going to get a big view when all he can do is work to feed a bunch of kids.
Mr. Hill	He just don't see very good yet. That's all.
Jake	Now I can tell you been drinking.
Mr. Hill	Why's that?
Jake	You start talking about big shit. We're just little people LT. That's all. It don't matter none. None of it.
Mr. Hill	I don't think so Gunny. Why else would you be over here with those clowns if it didn't matter.
Jake	That's the difference between me and you. If it was me I'd just leave him be, to work it out on his own. If he makes it, he makes it. If he don't then he don't.
Mr. Hill	Well aside from the big shit talk, I don't want anybody in my squad I can't depend on. Even if it's forking compost.
Jake	You wouldn't fork no compost pile.
Mr. Hill	I done my share before this.

Jake	What about now?
Mr. Hill	Reckon I would, if I had to. I wouldn't like it. But I'd go do it.
Jake	So, ol' Eddy there, he don't like giving up that LawnMaster or doing trim and bed work. But he's doing it. I think he's got more on the ball than you giving him credit for.
Mr. Hill	That's what I got to know. Just how much does he have on the ball. Hell, he don't even know hisself.
Jake	Well, you're the boss.
Mr. Hill	Listening to 'em go at each other just now, seems to me Perry's a bit edgy, too.
Jake	You reckon he's really a bastard? Seems to be a bit touchy on that point.
Mr. Hill	Yeah. I reckon he could be.
Jake	You used to have a place down his way. You know anything about him?
Mr. Hill	Hell, I didn't know every goddamn soul in the county.
Jake	Damn, LT. Don't bite my head off.

Mr. Hill   Sorry, Gunny. I'm just a bit twitchy. It's the rain I guess. Puts me back in mind of them hard times.

Jake   I been forgetting them times lately.

Mr. Hill   It's usually a long ways back there from here. Thank god.

Probably good to forget some of that crap.

Jake   But not the names. I been writing 'em down in here before it all gets too fuzzy.

Jake pulls a small notebook out of his shirt pocket and holds it.
Names and some things ought not get lost just cause your mind gets old.

Mr. Hill   (*finishes his drink and puts the glass down*) I better git. Got dogs to feed.

Jake   You and them dogs.

Mr. Hill   (*stands up, swaying a bit*) See you in the morning.

Jake   Yeah. You think about that Eddy.

Mr. Hill   Sure thing, Gunny. Don't drink too much tonight.

Mr. Hill walks out of the Yellow Rose and the lights fade to black.

Scene 3

*Early Monday morning in the university equipment workshop.
Francine, Perry, Steve, and Eddy sit around a wooden crate in the
center of the stage drinking their morning coffee. Jake is in the back
leaning on his work bench drinking coffee and watching the group. Mr.
Hill walks out of his office.*

Mr. Hill   Ok. Listen up. Today I want Perry and the Kid up at the center trimming the trees over by the north fence. They got a tournament starting up there tomorrow. I want that area squared away by this evening.

Perry   What about mowing around that parking lot?

Mr. Hill   Don't. They got a bunch of people up there today setting up. I don't want any problems with those folks over grass and dust blowing on 'em.

Perry   Yes sir.

Mr. Hill   Eddy, I want you to help Francine turn the compost pile this morning and after that I need you to get on up to the admin building and clear those flower beds. We got to get her flowers in the ground before the end of the week.

Eddy   I ain't turning no compost.

Mr. Hill   (*ignoring Eddy*) Francine, after Eddy gets the com- post done we need to get those flats ready to plant tomorrow.

LawnMaster

Eddy   I ain't turning no compost.

Mr. Hill   (*turning and moving toward Eddy*) That's the job
                  today.

Eddy   Not me.

Mr. Hill   You quitting?

Eddy   I ain't turning compost.

Mr. Hill   You better than everybody else? You too good to do
                  this job?

Eddy   No, I just…

Mr. Hill   You just what? You not going to do any dirty work?

Eddy   I do my share.

Mr. Hill   No, you don't. You're telling me you don't want to
                  get your hands dirty.

Eddy   That's not what I mean.

Mr. Hill   You saying that if you can't sit on top of some
                  goddamn machine you won't work? You afraid of
                  sweat?

Eddy   I ain't afraid…

Mr. Hill   You saying you don't want to do this job? You just want to be a pretty boy?

Eddy   I work damn hard…

Mr. Hill   You don't do shit, pretty boy. You just want to sit on a fuckin machine and look good. You don't want to work.

Eddy   I ain't no purty boy.

Mr. Hill   That's what purty boys do.

Eddy   I ain't no purty boy.

Mr. Hill   Sure you are. Always want to look good. Only wanting to do the glamour work.

Eddy   I work damn hard…

Mr. Hill   …When it gets tough you can't find their asses. Purty boys…

Eddy   …and I ain't no purty boy…

Mr. Hill   …just wanting to look good. Purty boys don't work.

Eddy   I work…

Mr. Hill   Bullshit. You just told me you didn' want to work.

Eddy   I said I didn't want to turn compost…

Mr. Hill   And I told you that was the job today.

Eddy   I ain't doing that.

Mr. Hill   Go home then. Every groundskeeper here done turned compost. Except you.

Eddy   I'm a equipment operator…

Mr. Hill   You ain't shit. Running a lawn mower ain't being an equipment operator. You got an operators license?

Eddy   No, but…

Mr. Hill   No buts, pretty boy. You ain't even a goddamn groundskeeper now.

Eddy   Wait a minute…

Mr. Hill   Get the hell out of my shop. I don't want anybody here I can't count on.

Eddy   I just don't want to turn compost…

Mr. Hill   You don't have a say. I need you to turn compost today. I don't have to explain why. If it ain't good enough to you that I need you to do it then get on. I don't need people in here second guessing what I tell 'em.

Eddy   I ain't second guessing…

Mr. Hill   You ain't doing. You got me standing here talking to you about why you won't do the job today.

Eddy   I just don't want to…

Mr. Hill   Hell, there's lots I don't want to do. But when the boss gives a direction…

Eddy   …This ain't no goddamn army…

Mr. Hill   You got that right. This ain't no goddamn army. Ain't nobody buggin out on me here. I got a small group of good people that don't get paid as much as they're worth. And everybody here depends on the other to do their job. No matter what that is.

Eddy   Shit…

Mr. Hill   You say you won't work. Then you aren't part of this squad. I don't have room for partway groundskeepers.

Eddy   I want to work…

Mr. Hill   I want you to work too. I need you on this squad. But I need you to pull your weight.

Eddy   But I don't want to turn no compost…

Mr. Hill   Then get. I got to have somebody I can count on day in and day out.

Eddy   I need the work…

Mr. Hill   Then go out there and help Francine get that damn
              compost ready. She needs it for the greenhouse.

Eddy   Up to now I always done what you told me…

Mr. Hill   (*loud and angry*) Bull shit. Just last month you took it
              on yourself to go mowing up by the parking lot when
              I told you not to.

Eddy   But it needed to get mowed…

Mr. Hill   You did more goddamn damage to that Mercedes
              than you're gonna make this year. You know, you
              don't listen. That's why you aren't up there anymore.
              I can't depend on you.

Eddy   It was a accident…

Mr. Hill   (*angry, forceful shouting*) That wasn't no accident. It
              was a probability. Why the hell do you think I told
              you not to mow up there. God damnit, you got to start
              doing what I tell you.

Eddy   I got it mowed though…

Mr. Hill   …Crap. The job that day was to *NOT* mow the
              goddamn grass.

Jake   LT, I don't think he's ever going to understand it.

Mr. Hill	(*normal tone*) Maybe you're right, Gunny. Eddy, you got a choice. Either help Francine with the compost or turn in your time sheet and go home.
Eddy	I gotta work.
Mr. Hill	Then go help Francine. That's the job today.

Mr. Hill motions for all of them to leave. Eddy and then Francine leave followed by Perry and Steve.

Jake	Well, LT. You pushed him didn't you.
Mr. Hill	A bit.
Jake	He didn't know you was sitting in the Rose last night listening to him say he wasn't going to turn that compost.
Mr. Hill	No, he didn't. But he's made his choice.
Jake	I don't know LT. You can't predict what that Eddy'll do.
Mr. Hill	For now he's doing his job. That's a start, anyway.
Jake	But he ain't smart. He still ain't figured out his job is just to do whatever it is you tell him. He's still got ideas of his own.
Mr. Hill	Wouldn't bother me if I trusted his judgment. But he doesn't think straight.

Jake	That's what worries me about pushing him in a corner like you did.
Mr. Hill	Time'll tell. You got some coffee over there?
Jake	Enough for a cup.
Mr. Hill	I'm ready for a refill.
Jake	I got some doughnuts over there too.

Mr. Hill takes his mug and goes over to the coffee maker.

Jake	Get you some doughnuts. That's good on a empty stomach. Helps cut the acid in the coffee.
Mr. Hill	You got to be kidding. Seems like the grease in those doughnuts would give you heartburn for sure.
Jake	Don't bother me none.
Mr. Hill	You got a stomach like boiler.
Jake	I like doughnuts. Not those cakey kind but those good ol' glazed ones. Some of them leave a kind of weird taste on the sides of you tongue. I think it's the grease they use.
Mr. Hill	Didn't know you were such a doughnut gourmet.

Jake

My momma used to make the best doughnuts. You got to use good lard to fry 'em in. You use vegetable oils you get that kind of odd taste.

Mr. Hill

Reckon you got a favorite shop too.

Jake

You bet. Salley's over on Bailey. Best ones in town. I could eat me a dozen for breakfast.

Mr. Hill

Damn. You're just a heart attack waiting to happen.

Jake

I ain't worried about it.

Mr. Hill

Not since Henderson?

Jake

Since then I don't worry much on prolonging things.

Mr. Hill

I hope you don't check out too soon.

Jake

I'm enjoying every minute long as I can. Pass me one of them doughnuts LT. All this talking is making me hungry.

Mr. Hill

Here you go. (*hands him a doughnut*) I got to go work on my bookkeeping. Maybe we should get some of these for the squad tomorrow morning.

Jake

They might like it.

Mr. Hill

How much are these things?

Jake   Six bucks a dozen.

Mr. Hill   (*takes out his wallet and gives Jake a 10*) Why don't
                        you pick up an extra dozen for the squad tomorrow.

Mr. Hill goes into his office. Francine sticks her head in the door.

Francine   Is he gone?

Jake   He's in his office.

Francine steps into the shop.

Francine   What was that all about?

Jake   He's just wanting Eddy to start following instruc-
                        tions.

Francine   It's not time to turn the compost heap.

Jake   Don't matter. It the principle of it that's important.

Francine   Eddy is real mad.

Jake   Where is he?

Francine   He's out there turning compost.

Jake   That's good then. He'll get over it. Eddy's ok. He just
                        has these ideas that don't work good in real life.

Francine   What makes you think he's gonna get over this?

Jake   He's got to feed his family. Probably can't afford any
                hitch in getting paid. He's illiterate remember? That
                purty much screws him.

Francine   I never think about it. He's good at getting by.

Jake   Yeah, he don't have many options.

Francine   I never heard Mr. Hill yell at anybody like that
                before.

Jake   He don't usually. He don't like to. That's why he was
                so mad this time. Want a doughnut?

Francine   No, thanks. I got to get back outside.

Jake   Eddy'll be ok. Might ought to give him some more
                time to cool off.

Francine   I left him out there. I got work to do in the
                greenhouse.

Jake   Well, don't let this bother you none. It'll all blow
                over in a day or two.

Francine   I'm not so sure.

Eddy walks in.

Eddy   You talking about me?

Francine   No. Not really.

Eddy	What the hell's that mean?
Jake	Your name come up but that was about it.
Eddy	What then?
Francine	Jake was just wondering…
Jake	…You eat doughnuts? Francine don't want none.
Eddy	They're good but I don't get to eat 'em much.
Jake	Go on then. Get yourself one.
Eddy	Thanks. Didn't get much breakfast.
Jake	Francine says you got that compost all taken care of.
Eddy	Yeah. (*quietly*) Wasn't much to it really.
Jake	That's right.
Francine	You know they teach classes in how to compost over at the Botanical Garden.
Eddy	Why?
Francine	It's not easy to get a good compost working.
Eddy	It's just a garbage pile.
Francine	No, no, no.

Eddy	What else is it then?
Francine	It's got to stay at the right temperature for the bacteria to grow. If it was just garbage all it would do is rot.
Eddy	Rottin's what it's doing.
Francine	Decomposing compost is different from rotting garbage.
Eddy	Sounds the same to me.
Francine	In a good compost pile you got a 30 to 1 mix of carbon to nitrogen…
Eddy	That's already more than I want to know. I got it turned like you showed me.
Francine	Good. The other thing on the list today was prepping those beds up by the admin building.
Eddy	I'm heading up there next.
Francine	Let me know if you need an extra hand.
Eddy	No, I can get it.
Francine	Suit yourself. I'll be working out in the greenhouse.

Francine leaves the shop.

Jake   How many kids you got?

Eddy   Five.

Jake   Damn. That's a few mouths to feed.

Eddy   They like to eat.

Jake   How old?

Eddy   My oldest is Greg. He's seven. Going into first grade
              this year.

Jake   He the one you was talking about the other day?

Eddy   Don't remember. I got two boys.

Jake   You was telling about him going over to that Davis
              mansion one time with your wife.

Eddy   Oh, yeah. That was Greg. Mrs. Davis liked him. He's
              a good boy.

Jake   He starting school this year?

Eddy   Maybe. Depends.

Jake   Want another doughnut? I don't have any business
              eatin them. They been saying it's bad for my
              cholesterol.

Eddy   Thanks.

Eddy eats another doughnut.

	He seems to be bright enough.
Jake	Be a shame if he missed out on it.
Eddy	Least he ain't having to chop cotton or pick fruit.
Jake	What's he do during the day.
Eddy	Help his ma.
Jake	She keeps house?
Eddy	Yeah. Sometimes she gets work keeping house for some of those rich women. He helps her at it when they got that kind of work for her. It's not much but it makes a difference.
Jake	Sure. Every bit helps. She sounds like a good woman.
Eddy	Yeah. She's from Tahlequah too.
Jake	Cherokee?
Eddy	Both sides.
Jake	Your kids got some strong Indian in 'em.
Eddy	They take after her.
Jake	Well I hope he gets a chance to go to school.

Eddy   Me too. We might go up to Oklahoma after this summer work is over and stay up there with her folks. They been saying they got some good schools for him up there.

Jake   Bet they do. Gets cold north of the river though.

Eddy   It's the ice storms I don't like.

Jake   Years ago I got caught up there one winter in one of them ice storms. Had a bull I was bringing back down for my dad. Truck damned near went off the road in a ditch. I hit a patch of ice. Shit. 'Course the rain was freezing to the windshield as it hit. I had to drive all the way back to Texas with my head hanging out the window just so I could see.

Eddy   When it's like that there ain't a damn defroster made that'll keep a windshield clear.

Jake   Once I crossed the Red River I was out of it. Made it all the way back to Tin Top without seeing any more of it.

Eddy   You get them storms down here.

Jake   Sometimes. But I don't think they're as bad as up in Oklahoma.

Eddy   I got to get going or Mr. Hill's gonna have another fit.

Jake   Hey, it's only a job. Just remember that. There's
                more to livin than this. You got kids. You know what
                I'm saying.

Eddy   No, not really. But thanks for the doughnuts.

Jake   Sure thing.

Eddy leaves the shop. Jake watches him walking away.

                Poor bastard. He don't stand a snowball's chance in
                hell.

Lights dim to black.

- LawnMaster -

Act 3

Scene 1

Late Thursday afternoon in the equipment workshop. Francine, Perry, Steve, and Eddy sit in the center of the stage around a wooden crate. Jake is in the back tightening bolts on engines and wiping down parts.

Perry	Almost time to get out of here.
Francine	Ya'll going over to the Yellow Rose tonight?
Perry	Not tonight. I got a date.
Jake	A date? It ain't the weekend yet.
Perry	It's sort of a different kind of date. We're going to that museum over by the coliseum.
Eddy	Damn. That's different. Don't sound like much fun.
Jake	Why you doing that?
Francine	Is that the Cézanne show?
Perry	(*confused*) I think so.
Francine	How'd you get tickets?
Perry	I didn't. The girl did. She had 'em.
Jake	Where'd you meet her?

LawnMaster

Perry	Up at the center.

Jake   Damn it. You weren't supposed to go associating
              with any of them women up there. Hell, LT told you
              already he didn't want you up there bothering any of
              'em.

Francine   What's her name?

Perry   Jill. Or June. J something. And she's the one that was
              bothering me…

Jake   Ain't likely.

Eddy   You don't even have clothes good enough to go to
              one of them museums.

Francine   This is a major touring exhibit. You got to wear a suit
              and tie. You got any clothes like that?

Perry   Not really.

Jake   How're you going to go to a suit party at the museum
              when you don't even have a suit?

Perry   She said she'd pick me up one.

Eddy   Hell, you sure this was real? Sounds to me like you
              was dreamin it.

Perry   Women like me. It's a gift.

Francine   I never noticed you had any gift. Something doesn't
               add up.

Jake   You better not be messing with any of them women
               up there.

Perry   I ain't messing with any of them women. It's a valet
               job. Sounded good though. Didn't it.

Francine   For a minute I was afraid you weren't lying or
               something.

Jake   Yeah, he damn near scared a year off'n my life that
               time.

Francine   Gift. Yeah you got a gift. I'm going to give you
               another gift of my boot up your butt.

Perry   Take it easy. I was just having a little fun with ya'll,
               that's all.

Steve   Yeah, fun, ha, ha. This place is just a barrel of fun.
               What I want to know what are ya'll going to do about
               the other morning? I haven't heard anybody
               discussing that.

Perry   What morning? What's got you all spun up.

Steve   Mr. Hill swearing at Eddy.

Jake   What the hell are you talking about?

LawnMaster

Francine	Why are you bringing that up?

Steve   Somebody ought to report it.

Eddy   Report what?

Perry   What's eating you, Kid?

Steve   You should report him to the school.

Eddy   For what?

Steve   Beating up that Pete guy. For swearing at you.

Francine   What are you calling swear? Mr. Hill doesn't swear. And he didn't beat up old Pete.

Eddy   He wasn't swearing at me.

Steve   I heard him. And shouting.

Jake   What you're talking about is a load of crap. I known LT a long time.

Perry   Jeez, Kid, calm down. You shouldn't be saying shit like that about Mr. Hill.

Steve   He made Eddy turn compost.

Eddy   Everybody turns compost.

Perry   Let it rest, Kid. Crap. It's almost time to get home.

Steve   You people…

Jake   Hell. Who are you calling "you people?" What's that
                 supposed to mean?

Eddy   Maybe the Kid ain't heard real cussing.

Steve   Stand up for yourself. You can't allow authority to
                 abuse you.

Eddy   Who wants to screw up a good thing?

Steve   I won't tolerate it. Somebody has to do something.

Francine   Maybe you ain't cut out to be a groundskeeper, Kid.

*Steve walks to Mr. Hill's office and opens the door. Jake and Perry
shout at him.*

Jake   Hey, Kid!

Perry   Kid!

Jake   Don't go in there!

Francine   What did he mean? What'd he mean by that?

Eddy   He's weird.

Mr. Hill's office door closes.

Francine   Well, he's gone now.

Jake   Like a junebug hitting a windshield.

Perry   You know what's the last thing to go through a bug's brain when it hits a windshield?

Eddy   No. What?

Perry   Its ass. Time for me to git.

Eddy   I think I'm going to stick around a bit and find out what happens.

Francine   I don't know if I want to know.

Jake   I reckon LT'll straighten him out. Or rip him a new one.

Perry   The Kid never did fit in. Did he? I could tell he's been wound tight about something for a couple of days. No idea what though. He don't say much all day.

Francine   He's one of them college kids. Easy life. Easy money.

Eddy   I bet this was the first time he ever had to work for a living.

Perry   I bet he's got credit cards.

Jake   You think?

Perry   Sure. He said he was working as a chemist before he got laid off. He had to be making some money.

Francine   I got one. Anybody can get one.

Eddy   But you and Jake's permanent. Me and Perry here, we're just seasonal.

Perry   I been in jail too much to get one of them things, anyway.

Jake   Perry, you got to stop getting thrown in jail. You getting too old for that shit.

Perry   I ain't been locked up since that time down in Laredo. Back in January.

Jake   You got to learn to pace your drinking. It ain't no good to chug that stuff.

Francine   All you guys talk about is drinking and bars and jail.

Eddy   I don't.

Francine   No. With you it's LawnMaster this and LawnMaster that. They got a lot more to life than that machine.

Jake   We was just talking about having fun. That's all.

Francine   Seeing some puke covered redneck passed out on the floor with his eyes frozen open doesn't match up with

	my idea of fun. You ever seen what ya'll look like drunk?

Jake

I don't get falling down drunk.

Francine

That you can remember.

Eddy

We didn't get that drunk the other night.

Jake

That's right. We just had a few beers after work and then them two went on home. A little buzzed but that was all.

Eddy

What do you think the kid is doing in there?

Jake

Don't know. It's kind of quiet in there.

Perry

How much longer you think they're going to be?

Eddy

Couldn't be much longer. I don't hear any yelling going on.

Perry

No shooting.

Eddy

Could be knives. That's quiet.

Francine

You and them knives. I'm getting. I don't need to hang around here waiting to find out what happened to the kid.

Jake

What do you think's happened?

Francine   I think he's quit. He doesn't have the stomach for this work. Really, he ain't a lawn boy. He's just a office boy.

Perry   Doesn't like for people to talk loud does he.

Jake   No. He seems to like things nice and quiet.

Eddy   What kind of work can somebody do that's like that?

Francine   Working in some chemistry lab somewhere I reckon.

Eddy   I couldn't stand that. I don't like being inside much.

Jake   I can't figure what he wanted.

Francine   Whatever it is it ain't here.

The door opens and Steve walks out.

Perry   Did he fire you?

Steve   No. I quit.

Eddy   Why would you do that? Mr. Hill's the best boss I ever had.

Francine   I don't get what your problem is.

Jake   Maybe this ain't as nice a place to work as what you're used to.

LawnMaster

Steve leaves without pausing. Everyone watches him.

Eddy   He's stupid.

Mr. Hill walks to the door of his office and stands there.

Mr. Hill   The Kid's decided this life ain't for him.

Jake   Damn.

Mr. Hill   What's the matter?

Jake   Francine won the pool. She said he wouldn't stick
                long enough to use the Bunton.

Eddy   What pool?

Perry   Yeah. We'd a cut you in but you were tapped out this
                week.

Eddy   Oh.

Mr. Hill   What'd you have, Gunny?

Jake   I said he'd drop out right after he started taking the
                Bunton down the slopes up at the tennis center.

Perry   I really missed on this one. I thought he'd make it to
                the first of the hot weather.

Mr. Hill   Looks like Francine took it then.

Perry   Time to git. I got to park cars tonight at the museum.

Eddy   I'm getting on too.

Francine   See you guys tomorrow.

Everyone except Jake and Mr. Hill leave the shop.

Mr. Hill   Been a hell of a day.

Jake   Yes, it has. In the end though I think it turned out for
               the best.

Mr. Hill   That's about all you can ask for.

Jake   Eddy seemed to have settled in.

Mr. Hill   I hope that helped him some.

Jake   I don't know. He ain't the brightest candle on the
               cake.

Mr. Hill   But he's loyal. I'll give him that.

Jake   Said you was the best boss he ever worked for.

Mr. Hill   After all that hell? Kind of sad when you think on it,
               if I was still the best boss he ever had.

Jake   He tries. So, what're you going to do about them two
               you lost this week?

LawnMaster

| Mr. Hill | Get some new ones. See you tomorrow. I got to go take care of my dogs. |

| Jake | Sure thing. See ya tomorrow. |

Mr. Hill leaves and the lights dim.

Scene 2

*Rainy Friday morning in the workshop, Francine, Perry, and Eddy sit
in the center of the stage around the crate. Jake is in the back.
Everyone is eating doughnuts and drinking coffee. Mr. Hill and Richie,
a new employee, walk in. They take off their rain gear and hang it by
the door.*

Mr. Hill   Ok guys. Here's the new kid. I got work to do.

      Gunny, you show him the ropes.

Jake   Sure thing.

Mr. Hill goes into his office.

Richie   My name's Richard.

Jake   Hey, Ritchie. You know how to play BooRay?

Richie   Richard. What's BooRay?

Perry   A card game we play when it's raining too hard to go

      out.

Francine   It's like spades. Five players is best but we get by

      with four. The guy before you didn't know how to

      play either. So he just watched.

Eddy   Want a doughnut?

Richie   Sure.

LawnMaster

Francine   Before the deal, you got to ante up. We play a one
                  buck ante. All antes go in the pot.

They all toss bills into the center of the crate.

                  The pot stays in the center until it's raked. What you
                  want to do is win the pot by taking more tricks than
                  anybody else. The other thing you want to do is burn
                  anybody you can.

Richie   What's burning?

Perry   When you ante up, anybody that didn't take a trick
                  has to match the new pot. That's when you lose your
                  ass. That's burned.

Francine   The deal rotates clockwise every hand.

Francine shuffles the cards.

                  The dealer shuffles and the person on the right cuts
                  the deck. Then you deal out five cards going
                  clockwise, one at a time and face down, with the
                  dealer's last card face up.

Richie   Sounds complicated.

Francine   Not really. Watch.

Lights dim.

> That's the trump suit for the round. A card of this suit always beats everything else.

THE END

LawnMaster

- LawnMaster -

Winter Crew

Characters

MR. HILL/LT - early 50s.

Grounds Dept Supervisor. Wears cowboy boots, jeans, shirt, and hat; clean, smoker, moderate drinker but not a bar room drinker, not a big talker.

JAKE/GUNNY - early 50s.

Small engine mechanic. Unshaven weathered face, khaki work clothes, looks like a heavy drinker.

FRANCINE - late 20s/early 30s.

Runs the greenhouse. Wears no makeup, worn blue jeans and tank top, tan from outside hard work, a bit grubby, tough.

EDDY - mid 30s.

Grounds keeper. Smoker, moderate drinker, illiterate, wrinkled khaki work clothes, pomade hair, red face from too much sun, abrasive personality, missing several teeth.

PERRY - mid 20s.

Grounds keeper. Ladies man, smoker, heavy bar room drinker, old blue jeans and polo shirt, flashy personality.

RICH/KID/BUD - early 20s.

New employee. New jeans and denim shirt, squeaky clean, no smoking or drinking, very middle class and out of place.

Setting

One week in the spring, fall, and winter of 1979 at a Texas university. When the crew is not out on campus working, they are gathered at the equipment workshop or sometimes in the greenhouse helping Francine prep the bedding plants. In the equipment workshop, Mr. Hill's office is on the right side. The door to the outside is on the left. In the center is a crate surrounded by four chairs and used as a table. At the back is a workbench with an old, grease stained coffee maker on it. Scattered around the area are leaf blowers, edgers, lawnmowers. The centerpiece of the equipment is a polished, gleaming riding mower - the LawnMaster.

Francine's greenhouse is her domain and it is brightly lit, clean and organized – unlike Jake's equipment workshop. Her tools are new and she seems to get more of the budget to buy what she wants and needs than Jake who is always working to keep things running as best he can. The greenhouse has a stack of flats in one corner for storing bedding plants, a workbench, and chair. She does not routinely have visitors in her shop.

- *Winter Crew* -

Act 1

Scene 1

Late spring afternoon. A thunderstorm has just passed over, one of the last rains before summer sets in. Richie and Perry are sitting in the cab of the Toro, a golf cart type of utility vehicle, parked outside the university admin building. Perry gets out.

Perry   Looks like that's about it for the rain.

Richie   What tools do you want?

Perry   A couple of rakes should do it.

Perry walks to a wall and sits down.

    This is where we sit. It's out of the weather and nobody can see you directly from the road over there.
(*Perry points to the left*)
Thing you always have to watch out for is Hill's truck.

Richie   What kind does he have?

Richie takes the rakes and bags out of the Toro.

Perry   A white Chevy. He comes round every now and then checking up on you. Ol' Pete never did get the hang of keeping a lookout for him. After Hill caught him over by the circle we had to find a different spot.

Richie   Eddy said Mr. Hill beat Pete up. Broke his hand.

Perry   That's what I heard.

Richie   Francine said it was a lie.

Perry   Francine takes up for him 'cause she's permanent. Same as Jake. The rest of us though just come and go with the season.

Richie   (*holds up the tools*) What do I do with this stuff?

Perry   Put those rakes over there and gim'e one of those bags. Always put some stuff in your bag just in case. If you get surprised, you can always show you did something and act like you're just picking something up. Like this.

Perry rolls over on his knees and stands up holding a paper wrapper that he puts in his sack.

Richie   I'm not that coordinated.

Perry   Practice. The other thing you got to look out for is that bastard Eddy. He'll rat you out if he sees you kicked back. Never trust that guy. He wants to go permanent. I think he ratted out Pete. But you never know. Anyway, we don't tell Eddy about these spots.

Richie   He's hard to get along with.

Perry   He's an ass. No education and lots of wannabe. God, he was pissed when Hill put Francine in charge up there at that tennis center. He still don't get it that he screwed up when he was mowing up there and sprayed that woman's car with them rocks. What a moron. Hill told him not to mow up there just then.

But Eddy, he don't listen to what he gets told. Last week Hill had to jump his ass again 'cause he didn't want to work for Francine.

Richie   How long has he been working here?

Perry   About as long as me. He might of started here a week or two before.

Richie   How long have you been working here?

Perry   A couple of years now, off and on. I first came up here from Marfa with ol' Pete. Pete was working down in Marfa on a place when I bumped into him. We got to be drinking buddies.

Richie   That's a long way from here. Ever wish you were back there?

Perry   I go back sometimes in the winter. My mom's still there. What about you? Where you from?

Richie   All over. Lived out in California mostly.

Perry   Damn that's a long ways off. What made you want to
                come over here?

Richie   I'm going to school here at night. This pays my
                tuition.

Perry   Jeez. Another one. Why the hell are you doing that?

Richie   So I can get a good job.

Perry   Job? What kind of job? This here's a good job.

Richie   I'm going to teach school.

Perry   Just what the world needs more of. Why in hell
                would you want to do that?

Richie   They need science teachers.

Perry   They need garbage truck drivers too. But I ain't'
                going to do it.

Richie   So, what are you doing?

Perry   When?

Richie   Instead of this.

Perry   There's nothing wrong with this.

Richie   But it's just taking care of lawns.

Perry   Shit. You ain't even done it yet to know what a groundskeeper is. They got to have groundskeepers as much as teachers. We don't get paid as much, but the hours are better. You actually know any teachers?

Richie   My uncle's a principal of a high school in Colorado.

Perry   Ain't the same. My momma's a teacher at high school, and I can tell you she worked a hell of a lot harder than the principal.

Richie   What's she teach.

Perry   You know you should try to be a principal. That's a hell of a lot better than being any teacher.

Richie   I'll think about it. What's you momma teach?

Perry   (*a beat*) Economics.

       She's a economics teacher.

Richie   What's your dad do?

Perry   Don't know. Never met him.

Richie   Oh.

Perry   I was real little when we moved out to Marfa.
                Momma was from Houston and she was gettin'
                away so he wouldn't bother her. So she moved us to
                Marfa and taught school. What's your folks do?

Richie   My dad's an accountant. Last I heard he was working
                at some refinery down south of Houston. Mom's a
                real estate agent. She's in California.

Perry   That's what you should do. Those real estate agents
                do real good. Why're you working on a grounds crew
                anyway if you got money like that? Hell, why don't
                you get your folks to pay?

Richie   I don't want them paying for any of it.

Perry   Whoa, hit a nerve there.

Richie   I'm just taking care of it myself.

Perry   Your folks divorced?

Richie   A few years.

Perry   Pissed at your dad?

Richie   We're just different that's all.

Perry   (*looks at him suspiciously and edges away a bit*)
             How different? What do you mean, different?

Richie   I didn't want to be an accountant.

Perry   Guess he thinks you ought not be a teacher either.

Richie   He said I ought to do something better than babysit
             kids for a living.

Perry   What was it you wanted to teach anyway?

Richie   Social Studies. Do you remember in *Catcher in the
             Rye*…

Perry   What's that?

Richie   Didn't you read that in high school?

Perry   I ran off when I was in junior high. Never went back.

Richie   You're kidding.

             Why'd you do that?

Perry   Bored.

Richie   Never went to high school?

Perry   What's wrong with that?

Richie   I don't know. I've just never known anybody that's
               never gone to high school. What'd you do?

Perry   Odd jobs. Kind of drifted around a few of the ranches
               out there near Marfa, working where I could. It's a
               good life except in the winter. It can get damn cold
               out there. 50 mile an hour wind blowing out of the
               north.

               One February I got caught standin out by the
               highway trying to hitch into El Paso. A big north
               came in blowing freezing rain and sleet. Down there,
               in that open country, if you're in the wrong spot,
               there's nowhere you can go to get out of the weather.
               I just had to stand out there and take it till somebody
               stopped and gave me a lift.

Richie   That's tough.

Perry   Sometimes, but most of it's been a lot of fun. To me
               anyway, but I don't reckon you'd enjoy it much
               though.

Richie   Probably not.

Perry   Hill's truck.

Perry rolls over on his knees and starts picking up leaves.

Quick. Get to picking up.

They immediately begin raking and stuffing their sacks.

Don't look around, just pay attention to raking the leaves and picking up the trash.

Richie   Ok.

Perry   I'll tell you when he's gone by. It's kind of tricky. If he see's you looking at him he figures you've been screwing off and he'll start watching you.

They work for a few seconds before Perry looks up.

Ok. He's gone by. Keep at it a bit longer though. Sometimes he'll drive up the road a ways and then turn around and come back to see if you're really working. Ol' Pete fell for that one.

Richie   What a jerk.

Perry   It's ok. He knows we work light. He just tries to keep us honest. Shit, here comes Eddy.

Richie   I thought he was supposed to be...

Pery   He never follows directions. That's why I told you to
              keep an eye out for him too.

Eddy walks in.

Eddy   What're you girls doing?

Richie   What we were told to do. See Mr. Hill?

Eddy   (*frantically looks around*) Where?

Richie   He just drove up the hill.

Eddy relaxes.

Eddy   I ain't worried about him. I got all those gutters
              cleaned.

Perry   Ain't you supposed to be down to the ag center.

Eddy   Stinks down there.

Perry   So.

Eddy   I ain't going to smell stink all day.

Perry   How'd you ever get hired for this job, anyway?

Eddy   I'm a equipment operator.

Perry   That don't say anything. All you know to do is turn a
             key and step on the gas. whooeee.

Eddy   Hell, I work backhoes and forklifts.

Richie   That's something we do a lot of?

Eddy   Don't let this slacker mess you up Kid. He's just a
             drifter.

Perry   Everybody here's a drifter. Except Francine and Jake.

Eddy   You think Francine is doing Hill?

Perry   Damn. What's wrong with you.

Eddy   She's always takin up for him. Mr. Hill this and that.
             I think she is.

Perry   She ain't doing anything like that. Hill's an old timer.
             What would she want with him?

Eddy   That don't mean nothing. Look at Jake. He's always
             going after them girls over at the Rose.

Perry   That's Jake. Besides, I'm more her type. Not Hill.
             Where do you get this stuff?

Eddy

Lets see. You and the Kid are out here in the rain cleaning up trash. He got me out cleaning gutters in the street. And she's sitting dry in the greenhouse.

Perry

Don't mean nothing.

Eddy

She never has to do this shit work.

Perry

Don't mean nothing. She takes care of the green-house.

Eddy looks down at Perry and Richie's sacks.

Eddy

Not much in your sacks.

Perry

Been fixing the sprinkler line. Remember?

Eddy

Oh yeah.

Perry

Why don't you get on over to the ag center where you belong. We got work to do.

Eddy

I ain't in no rush.

Perry

What'cha goin to do when Hill gets over there and can't find your ass? You going to wish you was in a rush then.

Eddy

And I ain't afraid of him either.

Perry   Tell that to your wife when he fires your ass.

Eddy   He ain't goin to fire me. I keep telling you people,
               I'm a equipment operator.

Perry   Duh. He don't need equipment operators. You're a
               groundskeeper, moron.

Eddy   Don't call me a moron, you bastard.

Perry   I ain't no bastard.

Perry moves toward Eddy.

Richie   Mr. Hill's coming.

Mr. Hill walks in.

Perry   Howdy, Mr. Hill.

Mr. Hill   Goddamn it, Eddy. I been driving all over this cam-
               pus looking for you. What'n hell are you doin over
               here?

Eddy   I was just checkin up on the boys here.

Mr. Hill   Don't you be worrying about them. You got those
               gutters clean?

Eddy   Yes, sir.

Mr. Hill   Then get on over to the damn ag center like I told you. Jesus H. Christ. They got leaves plugging up all the drains down there. They been calling me all morning about that.

Eddy   I was just on my way down there.

Mr. Hill   If you don't want to be a groundskeeper I'll get somebody else. Hear me?

Eddy   (*standing stiffly*) Yes, sir.

Mr. Hill   Go on. Git.

Eddy quickly disappears.

Mr. Hill   He's about as useless as tits on a boar hog.

Mr. Hill turns to Perry.

How're you boy's doing up here?

Perry   Fine. Just pickin up the leaves and such.

Mr. Hill   Ain't much in those bags. Got that sprinkler line fixed?

Perry   Yes, sir. It should be set up by now if you want to turn the water back on.

Mr. Hill   Ok. Ya'll go on over there. Call me on the radio
             when you're ready and I'll turn it back on. If it's still
             leaking let me know.

Perry   What'cha want us to do after that?

Mr. Hill   That's it for today. That should just about be quitting
             time.

             Tomorrow I'm going to put you up at the tennis
             center. If it works out, I'm thinking you'll be up there
             from here on.

Perry   Eddy's going to be pissed.

Mr. Hill looks at him, a bit surprised.

Mr. Hill   I don't want no more rocks going through any wind-
             shields up there. And I don't want somebody up there
             that don't follow orders. Got it?

Perry   Yes, sir.

Mr. Hill   Ok, then. I'm heading on back to the shop. Give me a
             call on the radio when you get back over to the
             sprinkler.

Mr. Hill leaves.

Richie   What do you think Eddy's going to do when he finds out?

Perry   No telling. Eddy's twisted in the head. You never know what that guy's thinking.

Richie   He is kind of scary.

Perry   Yeah. Let's get this shit back in the Toro and get over to that sprinkler line. I got to get that thing fixed fore Hill finds out it ain't been patched.

They begin loading up the Toro.

                     What're you going to do in the fall when Hill cuts us loose?

Richie   What's that?

Perry   When Hill cuts us loose.

Richie looks confused. Perry stops loading the Toro.

                     Didn't nobody tell you about the winter layoff?

Richie stops loading the Toro.

Richie   No one said anything about a winter layoff.

Perry   Shit. They didn't tell that other kid either. Ok, here it
            is. They only need a few groundskeepers through the
            winter, so, except for Jake and Francine we're just
            temps. Hill lays us off in the fall and keeps Jake and
            Francine on over the winter. That's why they're
            permanent and we ain't. Then right before spring he
            hires up a summer crew again. That's usually in
            March which gives us about four months off. Sort of
            like a vacation.

Richie   I can't take any vacation. I've got school. How'm I
            going to pay my bills?

Perry   That's what the overtime's for. You got to put by
            enough to carry you through for a couple of months.
            We got it good here. There's only a few months off.
            Me and some other guys head on down to the valley.
            We go over to Boys Town for a bit, kind of unwind
            after working all summer. You could tag along if you
            want.

Richie   I can't just take off and go down to somewhere else.
            I've got class this fall.

Perry   'Course you could get some other job around here
            through the winter if you don't want to head on out
            with us. You'd miss out on going to Boys Town,
            though.

Richie   Boys Town? Why would you go to Boys Town?
That's for orphans.

Perry   Not that Boys Town. You ain't never heard of Boys
Town?

Richie   I don't have any idea what you're talking about.

Perry   It's like a town of whores on the border down there,
over in Mexico. Across from Laredo.

Richie shrugs and shows no sign of understanding.

     You go across the bridge to Nuevo Laredo… They
got some good bars. You ever heard of Señor Frog?

Richie   No, I don't keep up with that kind of thing.

Perry   That's a good one. El Tiburon is another one. But
they don't have any prostitutes in downtown. That's
all over in Boys Town.

Richie   Is it legal?

Perry   Hell yeah, it's all legal. The Mexican government
runs it. Of course that's why you don't want to screw
up down there. They'll put you away real quick. I do
my heavy drinking back in Laredo. That way if I get

messed up at least I'm in a US jail. Those Mexican
jails are hard time, man.

Richie   Since when was prostitution legal?

Perry   Ever since I can remember. In Boys Town. It's not
really a town, you know. It's more like a
neighborhood or something. About six streets of
cantinas, restaurants, and whores, 6 maybe 7 miles
west of downtown. You make a couple of rights off
the main road out of downtown and it's right there on
the left.

Richie   You make it sound normal.

Perry   Hell, it's just a place. Cheap too, you can rent a room
at Celia's for 15 bucks, U.S. That'll buy you 12 hours.
'Course that's a rough room, not anything you would
probably stay in. My room didn't have any ac or toilet
seat. But hell, you ain't exactly there for that shit.
And if you stay in Boys Town you don't have to taxi
in and out all the time like everybody else.

Richie   Why would you go down there. Man, that's a ghetto.
If I was going anywhere like that I'd go to Las Vegas.

Perry   Vegas is for old folks, foreigners, and rich people.
None of it's real. Besides, Boys Town's not so bad.
The police control it all. They got a wall that's got

broke glass all on the top of it. Surrounds the whole thing so it's safe. The girls might lift your wallet but that's all. The only way in or out is past the police station. That's another reason why you don't want to get screwed up down there.

Richie   Let me get this straight. You're saying they have a walled off section of Nuevo Laredo, with broken glass stuck on the top of the wall so people can't go in or out unless they go past the police station?

Perry   Yeah. I guess that's about the size of it.

Richie   Reminds me of a Kafka story.

Perry   I don't know what all that means but that's why it's as safe as it is. Hell, if you were just out there loose in some little Mexican pueblo you'd probably get killed or something. I've heard stories about that action over in Tijuana. You got to think of it kind of like it's a party town.

Richie   That's not what I'm seeing.

Perry   Once you get past the cops and the jail, it's just like any other kind of strip. They got this green painted bar on the way in called the Shamrock but you want to get on past that and into the middle of town. The best stuff is in the middle. They got two kinds of girls, bar girls and door girls. The bar girls look the best since they work out of the bars but you end up paying two to three times more for them than a door girl 'cause you got a bunch of extra costs to cover. You got charges for the bar and the room and stuff like that. One of them could run you 30 or 40 dollars.

Richie   What's a door girl?

Perry   Them's the ones that have to stand outside by their rooms, waiting for you to come walking by. Some of 'em look good enough. The door girls are 10 maybe 20 dollars. But they got a lot of ugly ones too.

                Oh yeah, they got she-males down there too. Always make sure you know who you're playing with 'fore you get started, you know? Most of that is up in the northeast corner so you want to stay away from there.

Perry looks Richie over from head to foot.

                Unless you're into that kind of thing.

Richie   I'm not even sure I know what you're talking about.

Perry   You know, transvestites.

Richie   Oh. Not me.

Perry   Let's see, what else do you need to know…

Richie   …I've learned enough…

Perry   All the girls have condoms, but it don't hurt to carry
               your own. Most of them speak enough English to get
               by.

               Beer is cheap.
               Don't go down there when it's raining. The place
               turns to mud when it rains.

               Watch out for the two-girl routine. Any time two
               girls offer to do you for the price of one you can bet
               one of em's going to be lifting your wallet while
               you're getting preoccupied. Don't flash your wallet
               either. Any of them girls will lift it before you know
               what's going on.

               Being American in there don't count for shit, so you
               don't want to go around asking anybody about
               scoring some shit. Cops'll toss you in jail in a
               heartbeat and then ship you off to some federale
               prison.

               And don't argue with nobody.

               Oh yeah, stay away from the northwest corner where
               the New York Cantina is. That's strictly for the

Mexicans. Basically you want to hang out in the center where the Americans are. That's safest. And you can usually find a bar in there that's open round the clock, except on Catholic holidays or election day. You don't want to try to go in there then 'cause everything is closed.

Richie   That's bizarre. I don't believe it.

Perry   Which part?

Richie   The whole damn thing. You're lying. There's no walled off section of a town in Mexico, full of prostitutes. Guarded by the police. Run by the Mexican government.

Perry   Sure there is. Jake'll tell you. Ask him. Of course, most people stay in Laredo and catch a limo ride over, so he can't tell you much about staying over in Boys Town. Hell, you got to see it. The limos start showing up after dark and everybody party's till dawn. That's just the way it is.

Richie   Except for church holidays and voting day.

Perry   Right. Most all of 'em are Catholic you know.

Richie   The prostitutes are religious?

Perry   I don't know about church going but they do take their holidays.

Richie   I changed my mind. It's not Kafka, it's Dante. That's what it makes me think of. Dante's Inferno.

Perry   What's that got to do with prostitutes?

Richie   It sounds like Hell…

Perry   You didn't hear a word I was saying. It's a party town, man. It ain't Hell.

Richie   Sure I did.

Perry   You got it a little confused there, Bud. This here is about dirt poor women making a living and men letting off a little steam and having some fun. Everybody comes out fine. That's all it is. Drink some beer, have a bunch of sex. It's great time.

Richie   What you've been talking about's not poor women making a living. A poor woman making a living is more like them having to work in a sweatshop. Not being prostitutes having sex for money.

Perry   Which is worse? For the most part, those women there in the town are better off'n women out there sewing that sweatshop tourist crap 'round the clock.

You ever been around a sweatshop? You ever known
any poor people? They got no protection, no
medicine cept what they can get on their own…

Richie   Doesn't make it right.

Perry   What the hell do you know anyway. About what's
right and not right. Living in goddamn easymoney
California. You white assed Catcher in the Rye.
Damn. Forget I asked you, Bud.

Come on get in the Toro. We got to get on over to
that sprinkler line.

They get in the Toro.

Boys Town ain't no goddamn Inferno.

The lights go to black.

Scene 2

Early the next morning in the equipment workshop. Mr. Hill, Jake, and Francine are standing around the wood crate in the center of the stage drinking coffee.

Mr. Hill Francine, I'm going to move you back down here full time.

Jake What about the tennis center? You going to move Eddy back up there full time?

Mr. Hill No. I'm going to try Perry up there again. I been thinking on what you said and decided to give him another go up there.

Francine Eddy's going to get wound purty tight over that.

Mr. Hill I'm not worried about how Eddy's going to feel. God damn it. If he don't like it he can quit. I'll get another jackass to push that mower. Sorry Francine.

Francine Yes sir.

Mr. Hill Perry's worked up there before. He knows the ropes.

Jake I seem to recall some angry mothers calling you for about a month after you put him up there last time.

Mr. Hill   I already decided and now we're just going to play it
              out. Right?

Francine   Perry'll do ok.

Mr. Hill   He better.

Eddy walks into the shop.

Eddy   Whoa. What's up? Damn looks like something
              serious.

Mr. Hill   Nothing serious. Get yourself some coffee. We'll wait
              for the others to show up.

Eddy pours himself some coffee and stands by Jake.

Eddy   You guys hear about that guy that got killed over at
              Waldo's last night?

Jake   That was Wallace Johnson. I heard they been after
              him for about a week.

Mr. Hill   Who the hell is Wallace Johnson?

Jake   He's a fellow that owed some money to some boys
              over there in Dallas.

Perry walks in.

Perry   Shit, who died?

Mr. Hill   Get yourself some coffee. What time does the new
                         kid usually get here?

*Perry goes over to the coffee maker, pours a cup and stands by
Francine.*

Jake   Same time's everybody else. He should be here any
                         minute.

Eddy   Jake, how do you know about that guy getting
                         whacked over at Waldo's?

Jake   I heard it on the radio this morning.

Eddy   Oh.

Mr. Hill gives Jake a quick look. Richie walks in.

Mr. Hill   Looks like everybody's here.

Richie slowly walks up to the group.

Richie   What's going on? Did something happen? Is
                         something wrong?

Perry   No, Bud. We just all been standing around here
                         waiting on you to show up for work.

Mr. Hill   Ok. Listen up. I got to have Francine back down here full time now, so I'm going to shift some people around, temporary, until I can get somebody up at the tennis center fulltime…

Eddy   (*eagerly*)   I can do it. I been working here long enough.

Mr. Hill   …so I'm going to shift Perry up there for a while.

Eddy   (*protesting*) I been working here longer than Perry.

Perry   By a week.

Mr. Hill   That's enough of that. Eddy, you're going to pick up Perry's old assignment. That's the library and the buildings around the circle.

Eddy   Bullshit.

Mr. Hill   What's that?

Eddy   That's bullshit. That's all flower beds and weedeating and shit.

Mr. Hill   You had your chance up there at that tennis center and you screwed the pooch. Now you got trim work.

Eddy   Shit.

Eddy throws his gloves down.

Mr. Hill   'Cause you been here a couple of years I'm going to cut you one more minute of slack and let you pick them gloves up. You can't cut it, then get your crap and get out. I don't need no goddamn prima donnas on this squad.

Counting a couple weeks ago, this here is twice you ain't in step. You read me?

Eddy   I read you. But it ain't right.

Mr. Hill   Your minute's up.

Eddy   (*picks his gloves up*) Shit.

Mr. Hill   What's that?

Eddy   Nothing.

Mr. Hill   Ok. Perry, are you checked out on this LawnMaster?

Perry   Yeah, boss.

Mr. Hill   Kid, you take the Toro up there and Perry you got the LawnMaster. I want the Kid trimming boxwood and Perry you get the back forty cut. That ought to just about fill up your day. Ground might still be wet, so

be careful. I don't want any goddamn ruts in my
grounds out there. Now git.

Eddy   What about me, boss?

Mr. Hill   I got some trimming needs to be done. Got it?

Eddy   Yeah boss. I got it.

Mr. Hill   Good man. Ok then. Francine you need to check him
out on that.

Mr. Hill goes in his office, closes the door.

Eddy   That's bullshit.

Perry   You heard what the man said.

Eddy   If this was next month, I'd have just walked out o'
here.

Richie   What happens next month?

Eddy   City adds extra equipment operators on for the
summer. Pay's better too.

Perry   But they work your ass off. And it's hot. Least here
you can get in out of the sun when it's bad.

Eddy   Like hell. You don't get no breaks working here.
                That goddamn Hill sees to that.

Perry   Don't pay any attention to him, Bud. You just got to
                work smarter than numb nuts over there.

Eddy   Don't you cuss me. I'll cut you.

Perry   With what?

Eddy   You're making fun of me again. (*reaching a hand
                into his pocket*) I already told you to back off.

Jake   OK. None of that. Whatever you got, Eddy, keep it in
                your pocket. This ain't no jail house. Perry get your
                gear together and head on up to the tennis center.

Richie   What do you want me to do?

Perry   Hang on a minute, Bud. Let Eddy get out of here
                first.

Eddy   Francine, I ain't never done a bunch of trim work
                before.

Francine   Good time to start.

Eddy   So, what should I do first?

Francine   That's hard to say, Eddy. There're so many things I
             can think of. But I guess you ought to start trimming
             out the roses over by the girls dorm.

Eddy   Damn.

Francine   You know how to trim roses?

Eddy   Sure. I cut 'em back at home every winter.

Francine   This is trimming not cutting back. You ever trimmed
             roses before?

Eddy   I keep telling you people, I'm a equipment operator,
             not no yard man.

Francine   Jake, I'm going to run Eddy up to the dorm and
             check him out on trimming roses. Guess he's going
             to learn about being a groundskeeper after all.
             Com'on Eddy. Let's get a Toro. Grab them pruners
             over there.

*Eddy picks up a pair of pruning shears. Francine walks out with Eddy
trailing behind her. After they're gone Perry walks over to Jake.*

Perry   Say there, Jake. Mind giving me a hand on this
             LawnMaster? It's been a year or so since I last used
             it.

Jake   Thought you told LT you was checked out on this thing?

Perry   I am. It's just been a while and I don't want to screw anything up.

Jake   Ok. Wouldn't hurt to go over it with you.

He walks over to Perry.

                 Eddy has been kind of hogging the equipment. Don't guess you got that much time in on it lately.

Richie   What do you want me to do?

Perry   Just a second, Jake. (*He turns to Richie.*) Get one of the Toros out there and take it up to the center. Grab a couple of loppers and some shears.

Richie   What's that?

Perry   Those long handled things over there. You got your gloves?

Richie   Yeah I bought a pair last night.

Richie holds up a pair of decorated garden gloves.

Perry   Damnit. That ain't going to work. You need a good
                 pair of leather gloves. You'll get blisters for sure if
                 you use these things.

Richie   The leather ones were more expensive.

Perry   Don't ever cut yourself short on your tools. It's how
                 you make your living. For now anyway.

Perry takes a pair of gloves from his back pocket.

                 You can use mine till you get a pair you can work
                 with. See how they put the seam on these? No
                 blisters. These here garden gloves you got have a
                 seam right there on your thumb where you're going to
                 be gripping. See that?

Richie   Yeah. I see. But what are you going to use?

Perry   I got a spare set. Always carry a spare.

Jake   Com'on, Perry. I ain't got all day. This's about as bad
                 as trying to teach him to play BooRay.

Perry   Keep your shirt on, Jake. We're done. I'll see you up
                 there, Bud.

*Richie leaves for the tennis center while Perry and Jake stand by the
LawnMaster. Jake is holding his coffee mug.*

Jake   You like this work?

Perry   It's ok. How do you set the height of the blade?

Jake   (*points at a lever on the mower*) This lever. Shifter's
            over here. Fluidic drive so you ain't got no gears.

Perry   Yeah, I remember now.

Jake   Easiest mower we got to use. Lot easier than that
            Bunton.

Perry   That's the oldest mower we got.

            Say, why do you think Mr. Hill put me back up there
            at the center?

Jake   He wants to see what you can do this time.

Perry   You think he might keep me on permanent if I did
            good up there?

Jake   Possible. It's possible. But you got to watch yourself
            up there. That tennis pro is a mean sumbitch.

Perry   Yeah, Ol' Barksdale doesn't like me from the last
            time I was up there.

Jake   I'd steer clear of him then. Might ought to use that Kid for any business in their little club house. He's a college boy. Maybe they'll like him. And if they don't then it'll be him that gets the knife.

Perry   Yeah, that's a good idea. He ain't going to be sticking anyway.

Jake   How long you think he'll last?

Perry   Not long. I figure he'll find something else to do once the hot weather gets here. Inside where it's cool. That's what he's used to.

Jake   He ain't never worked outside before, has he.

Perry   Don't look like it.

Jake   I'm figuring he'll fold in three weeks. About the time he has to take that Bunton down the embankments at the tennis center.

Perry   Maybe, but that's what you said about that other one and he didn't even last out the week. I'm betting this one outlasts that. Same as last time, I'm saying it'll be when the temp gets up. First day over 100 and I bet'cha he gets another job somewhere.

Jake   Ok. I'll take that. Say 10 bucks?

Perry   You're on.

Jake   We ought to ask Francine if she wants in.

Perry   Yeah, she's always in on a pool. Why don't you ask
               her when she gets back from showing Eddy how to
               trim the roses.

Jake   What about Eddy?

Perry   No. Eddy got cleaned out again at cards the other
               day. Besides he'd tell if he knew, just to screw it up.

Jake   Ok, then. Another three way pot. That's 20 bucks to
               the winner. You can buy some expensive beer on 20
               bucks.

Perry   I'll just get a bunch of Shiner. I could get me a weeks
               worth for 20 bucks.

Jake   I'd get me a bottle of Maker's. Anything else you
               need to know about this here mower?

Perry   That's about it I guess. The rest I can figure out
               myself.

*Jake goes back to his equipment. Perry sits on the LawnMaster moving
controls and turning the steering wheel.*

Perry   You know Mr. Hill long?

Jake   Yeah, sure. Why?

Perry   You think he beat up Ol' Pete?

Jake   He didn't beat up anybody yet. Specially not Pete.
                Pete got beat up in the Rose.

Perry   You're shittin me.

Jake   No, I ain't. After LT caught him sleeping by the
                admin building he cut him loose and that night Pete
                got in a ruckus over at the Rose. Bashed up his hand
                and couldn't work no more.

Perry   I always heard it was Hill did it.

Jake   It was me that bashed up his hand. They was all
                covering for me.

Perry   Bullshit.

Jake   It was a accident. Pete got shitfaced and started
                bothering a friend of mine. Didn't mean to break up
                his hand, though.

Perry   Why didn't nobody ever say anything?

Jake   I'd be back in Henderson for sure. Maybe lose this
                job anyway.

Perry   So, Francine's right?

Jake   Purty much.

Perry   Guess I'll stop telling that story then.

Jake   But it does scare the new guys, don't it.

They laugh.

Perry   Yeah. It rattles 'em.

Jake   Even rattled some old hands as I recall.

Jake laughs alone.

Perry   Just makes you careful. That's all. So, that Steve quit
               for no good reason.

Jake   That's about the size of it. Not too bright for a college
               boy, was he?

Perry   'Course it was me that told him all about ol' Pete
               getting his hand broke.

Jake   Don't worry about it, none. He wasn't going to stick
               anyway.

Perry   I reckon not.

Who was your friend?

Jake

Juliet. That girl that hangs out over there. I was sweet on her at the time. Pete was drinking hard that night and tried to get friendly with her.

Perry

Remind me not to hit on any women you got a interest in.

Jake

Don't worry about me. We ain't got the same taste in women. I like 'em old and slow. Like me.

Perry

That ain't Juliet. So, what about Eddy? What do you think he's going to do about all this with me being up at the center?

Jake

Well, I thought he'd be more pissed than this. Looks like he ain't going to do shit.

Perry

Eddy's always talking about cutting people and stuff. But I thought he was gonna do something this time.

Jake

I known a few like that in my time. Nine times out of ten they just fold. Sometimes though they'll sit up an bite 'cha. Never know.

Perry

Yeah. Like them Post Office guys.

Jake   Never understood that. Course I never killed anybody
                I worked with.

Perry   You killed somebody before?

Jake   Only in the war.

Perry   Which one?

Jake   That was a long time back.

Perry   W W 2?

Jake   Hell, no. I ain't that old. Damn, I'd be dead by now if
                it was World War 2. Hell, no.

                Viet Nam.

Perry   What were you doing over there?

Jake   That question don't make sense.

Perry   You know what I mean. Were you in the Army?

Jake   (*spits before replying*) Hell no. I'm a Marine.

Perry   What'd you do?

Jake   (*doesn't look at Perry*) I was in the Scouts.

Perry   How many did you kill?

Jake   I don't remember stuff like that.

Perry   A bunch?

Jake   (*snaps*) You going to go mow that grass anytime
               soon?

Perry   I didn't mean to piss you off.

Jake   That's ok, boy. You better git on up to the center
               before LT comes out of his office.

Perry   Yeah. I already got plenty to do today.

*Perry bends down to turn the key. The sound of a starter motor turning
but the engine doesn't start.*

               Got a problem over here, Jake.

Jake   Did you choke it?

Perry   Yeah.

Jake   Might be flooded. It don't like being choked on a
               warm day.

Light dims to black with the sound of the LawnMaster failing to start.

Give it a rest. You'll run down the battery. Damn,

Perry. This ain't gettin off to a good start.

Scene 3

Late afternoon in the equipment shop. Francine and Jake are sitting around the crate in the center of the stage drinking coffee.

Jake   You get Eddy checked out on trimming them roses?

Francine   God. I'm scared to death he's going to leave me a bunch of mutilated bushes.

Jake   They'll grow back.

Francine   It's the shape I'm worried about. I'll have to replan the entire area if he butchers 'em too bad.

Jake   Maybe he'll do a good job.

Francine   Maybe we'll get hit by a asteroid too.

Jake   What asteroid?

Francine   You know, THE asteroid. Hit the planet. Wiped out the dinosaurs.

Jake   I don't keep up with that stuff.

Francine gets up, walks over to the door, and looks outside.

Francine   How do you think Perry's going to do up at the center?

Jake   He'll make out ok. Took him a bit to get the Lawn-
                Master going but he eventually figured it out.

Francine   Think Mr. Hill might keep him on full time?

Jake   Maybe. But Perry's a tumbleweed. He just can't stick
                long in a spot. I'm figuring he'll try but winter'll get
                here and then he'll be drifting back down to the
                border. Until spring. Long's he don't end up in
                Henderson he'll be back. He likes it here I reckon.

Francine   This is a good place.

Jake   It's not bad. Not bad at all.

Francine   What time is it?

Jake   About four, four-thirty.

Francine   To me, this is the saddest part of the day. It's the in-
                between time. All the work is done and most
                everything is shut down. But dark is still a few hours
                off.

                I can feel how quiet everything is getting. The
                secretaries in the offices close their desks and
                organize their papers, lock the doors. The students
                are back in their dorms. A few of 'em with late

classes are still in the buildings, but soon they'll be gone. It'll all be empty.

Jake   Well, in about a hour I'm gonna be sitting at the Yellow Rose with a glass of Makers, watching the news on the tv and eating little sausages.

Francine   That's an hour away. What about now?

Jake   I don't think much on them college kids so I guess it don't bother me none.

Francine   I got to go close up the greenhouse.

Francine leaves and Jake walks over to the door to look out. He doesn't see Mr. Hill come into the shop from his office.

Jake   Damn it. Now she said all that, it does feel kind of sad.

Mr. Hill   What's that, Gunny?

Jake   Nothing much, just something Francine was saying about how this time of day made her feel sad.

Mr. Hill   About what?

Jake   Don't ask me to explain it. Hell, I'm a mechanic I don't pay any attention to that feelings crap.

Mr. Hill   A damn good mechanic. Good lead man too.

Jake   I don't know that I was all that good at anything but
                  mechanicin'.

Mr. Hill   You always done what needed doing. Nobody asks
                  mor'n that.

Jake   Yeah. Guess you ain't going over to the Rose this
                  evening.

Mr. Hill   No. Not tonight.

Jake   Francine was wondering if you was going to bring
                  Perry on permanent.

Mr. Hill   I been thinking on it. Probably not though. Fall
                  comes and he's going to get itchy feet.

Jake   That's what I told her. That's about the time she
                  headed on over to her greenhouse.

Mr. Hill   She'll be ok. She's a tough one.

Jake   Smart too. This afternoon she started talking about
                  some kind of asteroid that killed some dinosaurs.

Mr. Hill   Yeah, Nova had a program on that last week.

Jake   What the hell is Nova?

Mr. Hill   One of those educational tv shows.

Jake   Figures. She's damn smart, a looker too. She don't
                wear any makeup so she looks kind of plain
                compared to Juliet over at the Rose. But, hell, she
                really don't need no makeup.

Mr. Hill   (*uncomfortable*) I never noticed. She's too young for
                old men like us.

Mr. Hill stands up.

                Well, I got to go make the rounds before they sleep
                past quitting time.

Jake   Perry won't. He's watching that clock no matter
                where he is.

Mr. Hill   You're right, but it'll still do 'em good to see that
                white Chevy truck making the rounds.

Mr. Hill leaves and the lights fade to black.

- Winter Crew -

Act 2

Scene 1

*Jake, Francine, and Mr. Hill are in the greenhouse after lunch on
Friday. They're standing around her workbench drinking coffee.*

Jake   Everything's so's I can't tell who all's doing
what any more.

Francine   He don't like change much for somebody in this line
of work does he.

Mr. Hill   He wasn't really cut out for it. Deep down he's a
rancher like his dad. But won't admit it. Spent his
whole life denying it.

Francine   How was it you got in the ranching business?

Mr. Hill   Me? That's a long story. It's not very interesting.

Francine   Was your dad a rancher?

Mr. Hill   No. He was a school teacher down in Houston.

Francine   Then how'd you get started as a rancher?

Mr. Hill   It's Jake's fault actually. He used to talk about it all
                  the time. He was in my squad. Kept saying how hard
                  a life it was.

Jake   Damn right.

Francine   In the Marines?

Mr. Hill   Yep. When I got out I thought I'd give it a try so I
                  started working for Groutman Cattle Company out of
                  San Antonio. Did that for some years. Then I leased
                  some land out near the Davis Mountains.

Francine   Perry was saying that's lonely country out there.

Mr. Hill   It was just me, so living out there was fine. Go in to
                  El Paso on the weekends when things got too quiet.
                  Or over to Marfa on Friday nights. But it's beautiful
                  country out there. Real peaceful. Stars at night like a
                  million pin pricks of light just arched over you like...
                  well, anyway it was a bunch of stars. In the day you
                  forget how things really are. But out there at night
                  you can remember how small the world really is.

Francine   Ain't like here.

Mr. Hill   No, it ain't. Hated to leave there. But the bank
                  wanted their money back so that was that.

Francine   You ever going to go back to it?

Mr. Hill   No. I don't reckon. I'll be too old by then. That's the
                    kind of thing you got to do when you're a young
                    man. And I did so there ain't no need to go back
                    down that road.

Francine   What'd you do in the Marines?

Mr. Hill   I better get back. Sorry to bother you with all this
                    talk. I better get back.

Mr. Hill turns to walk out.

Francine   (*calling after him*) That's ok. I was interested.

Mr. Hill leaves the greenhouse without turning around.

                    I think I must've made him nervous.

Jake   LT never was one to do a lot of talking about himself.
                    Not like that Perry. I like him enough though. Perry
                    that is.

Francine   Me too. He talks big but that's just his way.

Jake   Perry sounds tough but he wouldn't be any match for
                    LT in a real fight.

Francine   Why does everything with men got to end in being toughest in a fight?

Jake   You must mean, "people." I remember my second wife getting purty testy with a woman over who had the best taste in them purses.

Francine   Well I ain't.

Jake   If I told you SMU had a better looking landscape I think you might get a bit testy. Might even get try to out do 'em. Don't cha' think?

Francine   No.

Jake   Why is it you're putting in all them school colored flowers anyway?

Francine   You know that's something completely different.

Jake   I suppose so. Somehow.

Francine   It's not a personal contest. It's a professional thing.

Jake   Ol' Eddy there thought he was a professional equipment operator. But now he's just pushing a shovel. It ain't all personal contest for him.

Francine   You're just like 'em.

Jake   Not really. I don't care much about being profes-
                sional.

Francine   What do you care about?

Jake   I don't know. Maybe nothing.

Francine   Everybody cares about something.

Jake   Most times I just want to be left alone, I reckon.

Francine   That's something.

                You ever been down to Glen Rose?

Jake   I been by Comanche Peak.

Francine   At Glen Rose they got dinosaur footprints in the
                rocks.

Jake   Is it one of those scam things?

Francine   No. It's real. They got a state park built around it.

Jake   No, I never been over that way.

Francine   They got these dinosaur footprints in the creek bed
                down there. And you can see where they was walking
                across the mud flat.

Jake   I don't know, Francine. I never could understand how
                something like mud could get turned into a rock
                without getting washed away first.

Francine   I think it was the asteroid. I think when it hit, the heat
                from it baked the mud in a instant. And then there
                wasn't any rain for a long time. They had a show on
                Nova all about it.

Jake   Sounds like a one in million chance to me.

Francine   That's about the odds of my roses not looking like
                hell once that Eddy gets done with 'em.

Jake   Maybe.

                You know, you're smart.

Francine   For a groundskeeper?

Jake   For anybody. That's about the only smart
                conversation I ever had here. Sometimes at
                Henderson you'd run into somebody that was smart
                and you'd wonder what the hell went wrong for them
                to end up in there.

Francine   What went wrong for you?

Jake   Damnit. I stepped into that one didn't I?

Francine   All this time I been nice and never asked. So? What
            was it went wrong?

Jake   Seems to be my day. Ok. But you don't tell anybody.

Francine   Promise.

Jake   I was married to this addict once. Went through
            everything I had. Cleaned me out. One day I come
            home and she's sleeping with this bastard. So I beat
            the shit out of him. Didn't kill him though. But I
            fixed him good. I got some time cause of that.

Francine   Jeez.

Jake   So that's it.

Francine   Sorry I asked. I figured you robbed a bank or some-
            thing.

Jake   Naw. That's too romantic. Besides I'd still be at
            Henderson working on the farm if I did that.

Francine   What happened to your wife?

Jake   That one ended up down in Houston somewhere last I
            heard. She couldn't kick it and I never heard anymore
            of her. Probably dead by now.

Francine   How many times you been married?

Jake   Too many. I'm a weak man. You?

Francine   None. I almost was married once. But I got out of it
at the last minute.

Jake   Smart girl. It ain't all it's cracked up to be. Once you
say "I do" everything about it changes. Don't know
why that is. It just does.

Francine   Bill couldn't stop partying long enough to keep a job.
So I put up with the rest of it.

Jake   What you mean, "rest of it?"

Francine   Being a single woman who ain't a teenager no more.
It looks like fun on tv shows but it gets old. I'm used
to it. And I have my cockatiel.

Jake   You got you a parrot bird?

Francine   Sure. But it's not a parrot.

Jake   No cat?

Francine   Watch it.

Jake   Most women I know like cats.

Francine   That's a stereotype.

Jake   No it ain't, I know 'em. Like Juliet over thare at the
              Rose.

Francine   Anyway a cockatiel is better. It actually cares about
              you. I never warmed up to cats. They're just
              'masculated substitutes for a man.

Jake   That was a insult. I think. Wasn't it?

Francine   Well that's the way they are. Kind of come and go on
              their own. Not really attached to you 'cept when it's
              time to eat. And they only like you on their terms. I
              had enough of that without gettin me a animal that
              was the same only smaller.

Jake   But, how'd you settle on a cockatiel?

Francine   I was in a pet store once when they had some hand
              raised baby cockatiels. They were just the sweetest
              things. You ever been around one?

Jake   No. Don't think I ever been in a pet store. Sure ain't
              been around no cockatiel.

Francine   You only want a hand raised one. Not one of those
              wild ones they bring in. I feel sorry for them. They

shouldn't sell them. They're wild and never associate with you. But the hand raised ones are different.

Jake   That's good to know.

Francine   I can tell you're all excited about it.

Jake   That's ok. I never cared much for animals.

Francine   But, you grew up on a ranch.

Jake   More like a dirt farm with cows than ranch. And that was my dad wanted that. Me, I was just born there. All us chaps lit out of there first good chance we got. You ever live on a farm?

Francine   No. I grew up in town.

Jake   Taking care of them animals'll cure you of wanting any.

You know, they had a massacre just east of Comanche Peak back in the 1800's.

Francine   No, I didn't.

Jake   There's a little creek east of the peak. Runs into the Brazos on down from there. Five or six settlers got killed by the Indians on that creek.

Francine   That's not a massacre.

Jake   Sure it was. That's really about all the people that
                ever got killed at a time. 'Course when you only got a
                few hundred in the whole damn county, killing five
                or six was a hefty part of the population.

Francine   A massacre should be something like hundreds of
                people getting killed.

Jake   That would be Hollywood.

Francine   I never cared much for history.

Jake   You knew about that there asteroid.

Francine   That's science. Science is different. History is just
                peoples memories. You can't know anything by that.
                It's always getting changed, depending on whose
                remembering's getting told.

Jake   So's science.

Francine   What?

Jake   So's science. Just depends on who's story you want
                to believe.

Francine   You can measure in science.

Jake   Science just tries to explain to folks what thing just
                        happened. That's all. Gives frightened little people
                        answers to cling to in the dark.

Francine   I ain't frightened.

Jake   I didn't mean you in particular.

Francine   So what's history?

Jake   It's the stories of what was.

                        Like them people that got killed by the Comanche
                        down in that creek.

Francine   Or them dinosaur footprints.

Jake   There you go.

                        I guess I better get back at it. LT'll have 6 fits if he
                        finds out I done spent my day chitchatting with you
                        here. Been a good talk though. I enjoyed it.

Francine   Me too, Jake.

Jake leaves the greenhouse and the lights fade to black.

Scene 2

A mid-summer Tuesday afternoon in the greenhouse. Francine is alone, working with the plants, potting cuttings, planting seeds, watering, etc. when Richie walks in.

Richie	Hey, Francine.

Francine looks up, surprised to hear someone in her greenhouse.

Francine	What'cha doing over here.

She looks back down and continues working with the plants and pots.

Richie	Grounds work is all caught up so I figured I'd come over and see what you were doing.

Francine	Just getting some cuttings potted. They're going to go in up at the library.
	Does Perry know you're over here?
Richie	I guess. He's over in the shop talking to Jake. Nice place you got here.
Francine	Thanks. I like it. It took me awhile but I finally got it like I want it. I got my work table here.

She points at a stack of trays by the wall.

Replacement flats are over there.

She points across the room at a group of ferns and potted plants.

Office plants I got over there.

Richie   Nice colors.

Francine   School colors.

Richie   Huh?

Francine   School colors. You know, like the school mascot and
                all that.

*She continues working on the flats while Richie wanders around look-
ing at the greenhouse.*

Richie   I never paid any attention to it.

Francine   You like going to school here?

Richie   Sure. It gets a little rough though, after working in
                here all day. What about you? You ever take any
                classes here?

Francine   No, not here. But I went to junior college for a while.

Richie   What were you studying?

Francine   Nursing. I was thinking about being an LVN.

Richie   So what happened? Change your mind?

Francine   Ran out of money.

Richie   Couldn't you get a student loan or something?

Francine   I didn't qualify.

Richie   (*puzzled*) I thought anybody could qualify.

Francine   Well, I don't. I don't want to talk about this.

She points at a bag behind Richie.

          Hand me that bag of potting soil.

Richie   Sure.

He turns around, picks up the bag and hands it to her.

          Well, you got a good job here anyway. That's
          important. Hey, you could retire here.

Francine   Yeah. And I got my greenhouse and the landscaping.
          I guess I'm happy.

Richie   (*he looks at Francine, grinning*) I wasn't talking
          about being happy. I was talking about having a good
          job.

Francine   You've been here a couple of months now. Are you
                happy?

Richie   I never think about it anymore. Being happy's not
                one of my priorities.

Francine   Worst mistakes I made was when I was being happy.

Richie   So when are you putting those plants in the ground?

Francine   This fall. It's too late for summer, hot weather's here.
                Supposed to hit 110 tomorrow.

Richie   You know, that's the hardest part about this job.

Francine   Secret to this summer work is you have to get as
                much done by 10 as you can. It'll be getting up over a
                100 not long in the day after that.

She cleans her tools.

                Tomorrow you ought to bring a thermos of cold
                water. Use it to keep your head wet. That's how Perry
                and Eddy get through the heat.

Richie   Perry doesn't like me, you know.

Francine   I wouldn't worry about it. Mr. Hill is the one that runs
                this place, you just worry about him.

She puts her tools away and begins to clear off her table.

Perry may change his mind later, after you show you can do this work. Some people come and go here too quick to care about.

Richie   Ok, I'll give it some time.

He helps her stack the flats with potted plants.

You know, I figured you were going to say you were studying to be a botanist or something. I wasn't expecting you to say you were studying to be a nurse.

Francine   No, I never thought about studying to be a botanist.

Growing up, we didn't have much money so I was trying to get me a good paying job. My dad, he was a mechanic, a car mechanic. And my mom, she was a waitress. Momma, sometimes she'd say that if I was a nurse maybe I could get to meet a doctor that away and get married. She was hoping I could do better, you know?

Richie   They sound like good people.

Francine   They were. Worked real hard. But they're dead. About three years now. First, dad, he had a heart attack right there in his shop and (*she snaps her fingers*) that was it.

Richie   That's sad.

Francine   He was lucky. Mom, she got that pancreatic cancer. All they did was sew her up and send her back home with a bunch of pain killer. She lasted a couple of months. Pain was so bad, after a month the pain killer just didn't work. Me and my sister had to sit up with her when she got back until she passed. It was a rough time.

Richie   Jeez.

Francine   So I moved up here to get a new start.

My sister ended up waitressing at a joint in Amarillo. She married, got three kids, and then got divorced. I wouldn't have that life for nothing.

Richie   You've done pretty good.

Francine   I get by. That's about all anybody could want.

Perry walks into the greenhouse.

Perry   Hey Bud, I been looking for you.

Richie	Looks like you found me. I've been in here helping Francine. Grounds work is all done.
Perry	You should've checked in with me first.
Richie	You were talking to Jake. Besides I'm done for the day.
Perry	You ain't clocked out yet, Bud.
Richie	Nothing's going to happen in five minutes.
Perry	Mr. Hill wants us to fix a leak up at the center. You're on overtime now.
Richie	Not me, I have class in a few minutes. You'll have to do it on your own or wait till tomorrow morning.
Perry	That class can wait. We got a broken line to fix.
Richie	You got it turned around. The line can wait. Class starts in about…

Richie looks at his watch.

	…fifteen minutes.
Perry	You want me to tell Mr. Hill you refused to fix that line?

Richie   No. I'll tell him. I don't want it to get screwed up in
                translation.

*Richie leaves the greenhouse with Perry trailing behind him. Perry
continues talking as they walk away.*

Perry   You know this ain't no country club you belong to.
                This here is a real job… you can't just come and go
                as you please. You got to check in so we know where
                you are…

*Francine's cell phone begins playing a tune. She walks over to her
purse and takes it out.*

Francine   Hello… Oh, hi… They're both on their way over…
                Perry really doesn't like that new guy… I don't have
                any idea… I told him to give it time… Not Perry, the
                kid… He seems ok to me… What do you want for
                supper?

She sits in a chair by the front door.

                I'll have to get some on the way home… No, it's no
                problem… I don't mind… Oh, he's got class in a few
                minutes and doesn't want to go back up to the tennis
                center today… Like I said, him and Perry ain't getting
                along… Ok, I'm locking it now. I'll be over in a
                second.

*She turns off the phone, but remains sitting in the chair looking out the
door. Eddy's voice shouts from off stage.*

Eddy   What'cha doing Francine?

Francine   Waiting for quittin time. What are you doing?

Eddy   Just putting up the tools.

Eddy walks into the greenhouse.

Francine   How're the pyracantha doing over by the liberry?

Eddy   Ok, I reckon. I don't mess with 'em much. Them
                damn thorns can go right through your gloves.

Francine   I think I'll go up and take a look at them tomorrow
                morning.

She stands up and walks over to pick up her purse, puts the phone in it.
                They don't need much attention. I forget about 'em
                sometimes.

Eddy   You ok, Francine?

Francine   Sure. How'er the kids?

Eddy   Doing fine. They up at my wife's folks this week. It's
                good up there. Lots of country to run around in.

Francine   I heard Jake say her mom lives up in Tishomingo?

Eddy   Yeah. You know my wife and me's from just east of
                there.

Francine   No, I didn't.

Eddy   That used to be Indian Territory, before it got turned
                it into Oklahoma. Made a damn musical out of it.

Francine   Hell, Eddy. I never heard you talk like that before.

Eddy   Sorry.

Francine   No, no. That's great. So, you're Indian?

Eddy   On my momma's side. But I don't fit in up there.

Francine   Nobody really fits in anywhere. They just pretend
                too. Some pretend at it harder than others do. Some,
                like you don't even try. But you're honest and to me
                that counts for more than if you was pretending.

                D'esperance.

                Let's get on up to the shop. It's just about time to
                clock out.

Eddy   Yes, ma'm.

*He leaves the greenhouse and Francine follows him. She turns out the
light, closes the door, and locks it.*

Scene 3

In the Yellow Rose, a bar near the university, outlaw country western music is playing in the background, Willie Nelson, Blue Eyes Crying in the Rain, Crazy, and Seven Spanish Angels. Jake and Perry are sitting at a table drinking beer and talking, pitcher of beer and basket of pretzels are in the center. The bar is dark except for the center spot on Jake and Perry.

Jake   Why don't you go to school here. Like the Kid. He said it don't cost nothing as long as you're working here.

Perry   I don't have time.

Jake   I don't know about you, but time's all I got a lot of. You know?

Perry   I hear you.

Jake   You ain't got no kids. No wife. You have a fulltime girlfriend?

Perry   Not regular.

Jake   Then you ain't got nothing in your way.

Perry   Sounds simple don't it.

Jake   Most things are when you cut 'em to the quick. Peo-
                ple just adds in the decorations to make life compli-
                cated.

Perry   My life's pretty simple.

Jake   There ya go. Least ways, you ought to look into it.

Perry   What'd your folks do?

Jake   Small time farming and ranching.

                The Brazos cut through there, so it was purty good
                land in spots if'n you got some water.

Perry   Bet it got hot out there in the summer.

Jake   You got that straight. Just like here. Damn wind
                comes up off the Chihuahua and your skin feels like
                it's just going to shrivel up. Like one of them
                Egyptian mummies.

Perry   Live out there all your life?

He pours some more beer in his mug.

Jake   Not hardly. I got away from there as soon as I could
                get.

Perry   So what'd you do when you got away from home?

Jake   Went in the Corps for a spell.

Perry   Did you like it?

Jake   It wasn't like in a TV show.

Mr. Hill walks out of the dark with a mug of beer.

Mr. Hill   I wondered where you got to.

Jake   Hell, you know'd where I was. Question is, what're you doin in here. I don't reckon I seen you in here for a month or more.

Mr. Hill sits down at the table with them.

Mr. Hill   Oh, I just thought I'd swing by and get me something to drink 'for heading home.

Jake   That sure aint normal. Something wrong?

Mr. Hill   No, nothings wrong. I just ain't been in here lately. Wanted to see if they was still serving beer and playing country music.

Perry   That old outlaw music.

Jake   Nothing wrong with that.

Perry   Didn't say there was. But there's other kinds of
               country music now than this.

Jake   But this here's true music. Not that electronic shit.

Mr. Hill   Damn, Perry. You done got him started now.

Jake   Damn right.

*The three sit at the table drinking beer and eating pretzels while Willie
Nelson's music continues playing and the light dims to black.*

Act 3

Scene 1

A fall Friday morning in the shop. Francine, Perry, Richie, and Eddy are sitting in the center of the stage around a crate. Jake is in the back tightening bolts on engines and wiping down parts.

Eddy   You think today's the day?

Perry   More'n likely.

Richie   Day for what.

Eddy   Day Hill pulls our plug.

Richie   Why today?

Perry   Grass is going dormant and we got the last of it cut yesterday.

Eddy   I really got screwed this year on usin the LawnMaster.

Perry   You shouldn't never have put them rocks into that woman's windshield.

Eddy   I was just doing what I was getting paid to do.

Jake   You ain't never figured out all season, the only thing
              you was paid to do was what LT told you to do.
              Nothin more. Nothin less.

Eddy   That's what I done.

Jake   Eddy, Eddy, Eddy.

Francine   Jake's trying to tell you that you got to listen to what
              Mr. Hill told you every day and then do that. But you
              keep on hearing what he's saying and then doing what
              you think he should of told you. That ain't the same
              thing.

Richie   What are we going to do if it is today?

Perry   Sleep late tomorrow.

Eddy   I'm heading on up to Tishomingo for the winter.

Perry   Why the hell are you going north in the winter time?
              All them ice storms up there?

Eddy   My wife's got family up there. Probably get me a job
              up there running a forklift at lumber yard or
              something. I'm a equipment operator, I ain't no
              grounds keeper.

Perry   I noticed. Say there, Francine, how long you think it's
               going to take those roses to come back.

Francine   Don't pay any attention to him, Eddy. You done purty
               good for trimming 'em first time. Next year you'll
               have it down.

Eddy   I been thinking about staying up in Oklahoma next
               year. I got my kids in school and all. It's time I was
               settling down some. That's what Sue's been saying.
               Besides I ain't no groundskeeper. I'm a equipment
               operator.

Jake   Smart move. Take care of them kids.

Perry   Damn. You're going to break up our group here.

Eddy   You never liked me anyhow.

Perry   That ain't true. We just don't have nothing in common
               that's all.

Francine   I hope it works out for you, Eddy.

Jake   What's with everybody today? Nobody's got let go
               yet.

Perry   Hey, Bud. What're you going to do about your going
               to school and all once he cuts you loose?

Richie   I'm trying to get on at the library.

Perry   Figures.

Eddy   Why would you want to work in a library? You can't be outside or anything. That ain't going to last.

Richie   It's year round. That way I don't have to worry about shifting jobs every winter.

Perry   He ain't like you, Eddy. Bud here likes to be inside. He don't like being out in the weather.

Richie   That's not it. I can't just take off in the winter and go off somewhere else like you guys can. I'm going to school.

Perry   That's right he's studying to be a…

(sarcastically)

                …junior high school teacher.

Jake   I wish I'd had a good teacher when I was in school.

Eddy   That's all you people talk about. There's a hell of a lot more to life than going to school.

Richie   Like operating equipment?

Eddy

Hell yeah. At least it's doing something. Ain't no school teacher going to learn you how to work a backhoe or a forklift. That's what pays the bills. Not no social studies or whatever the hell it was you going to try to teach them kids.

Richie

I'll keep that in mind.

Eddy

You been so busy this summer going to that night school you ain't learned nothing about working. This here's the real world. Not some little school room somewhere. That's what you ought to be teaching them kids, but hell you don't know nothing about it. Even after all this a time.

Richie

They go to school so they can choose what they become. That's what school's all about, so they don't have to be equipment operators…

Eddy

Who wouldn't want to be a equipment operator?

Richie

…or groundskeepers or mechanics.

Perry

You still don't get it, Bud. Eddy is telling you that in the end all that schooling don't really change nothing.

Mr. Hill walks into the room from his office.

First you're born then you die and in the middle it's all…

Mr. Hill   Everybody here?

Jake   They all think yo're going to let'em go this morning.

Mr. Hill   Yeah, it's time. I got to cut back to the winter crew.

Perry   Damn. Looks like we're going to be sleeping late tomorrow, boys.

Mr. Hill   I wish I could keep you all on through the winter, but you know how it is. I only got so much budget to work with. I got your checks here…

Mr. Hill pulls three envelopes from his shirt pocket.

Eddy, this one is yours.

He hands an envelope to Eddy.

Hope you make it back this way next March.

Eddy   Maybe so Mr. Hill.

Mr. Hill   Perry, this is yours.

He hands an envelope to Perry.

Sorry I couldn't keep you on permanent. Maybe next
year things'll work out for you.

Perry   That's ok. I been looking forward to the time off.

Mr. Hill   Where you headed now?

Perry   Same as every year. Laredo, Mexico, maybe out to
Los Angeles. I ain't decided yet. Just going to let the
spirit move me. Like always.

Mr. Hill   Stay out of trouble this time. You don't need to be
spending any more time in jail.

Richie, this envelope is for you.

He hands the envelope to Richie.

You did good up there at the tennis center.
I got a call from the ladies up at the library about you.
They want you to start on Monday up there, if you
want to work up there.

Richie   Sure I do.

Mr. Hill   It's not as good working down here, but it'll help you
pay your bills till I staff back up next year.

Winter Crew

Perry   Betcha Bud don't make it back down here next year.

Mr. Hill   Never can tell.

He turns to Jake and Francine.

                 Jake, you and Franie'll get your checks same as usual.

He turns back to Eddy, Perry, and Richie.

                 Ok, you guys. That's it.

He waves them toward the door.

                 Might as well head on out of here. Don't forget to
                 swing back this way next March.

Eddy, Perry, and Richie leave the shop, waving as they walk away.

Mr. Hill   Hope they stay out of trouble this time.

Jake   Aint likely.

Francine   LT, I don't think Eddy's going to make it back next
                 year.

Mr. Hill   I think yur' right. (*he pats Francine on the shoulder*)
                 Hope he does ok up there.

Jake   Well, we got more'n we can do now.

The lights dim and a Willie Nelson song, Pancho and Lefty, plays.

The End

- WTexas in 2 Plays -

LawnMaster, began life as an assignment for a playwriting workshop led by Amy Freed at Stanford in 2002. In its original form, it focused on the Kid's entry and exit from the alien (to him) world of the grounds crew, but as the piece evolved, the more dynamic story became that of the "regular" employees. The second work, *Winter Crew*, begun after completing the workshop at Stanford, continued the narrative of the "regular" employees in *LawnMaster* as they finished the summer work season. During the development of this piece, the importance of Mr. Hill, the head of the grounds crew, and his relationship with Jake, his old buddy from the Corps, became a theme. Later revisions of both pieces further reduced the importance of the Kid to the true narrative line and emphasized the importance of Francine as the rational glue that binds the crew as a unit.

The basis for these pieces was a brief period of time when I worked on a university grounds crew. While the characters and events in these two plays are works of fiction, I have actually driven a Toro utility vehicle, operated an ancient Bunton mower, picked up trash, dug real ditches, and trimmed shrubs for a living. Thanks to Pete who taught me how to dig ditches all day. I lasted until the hot weather.

The final form of these two pieces began to take shape in 2008 after reading Cormac McCarthy's *the Sunset Limited* – that of a narrative in dramatic form. The pieces were reformatted from a standard script style and format into a more easily read narrative form like that used in *the Sunset Limited*.

When I was growing up, my mother taught Senior English in high school and one of the main activities of her senior classes was producing and performing in the "senior play." Each year, she would bring home sample play books which she received from publishers and I read them as though they were novelettes. The idea of narratives in dramatic form has been with me from the time that I began reading.

CGW

Clifford Wayne received his MFA in writing at the University of San Francisco, is a member of the Association of Writer's and Writing Programs, the Alabama Writer's Forum, and is currently working on his PhD at the University of South Alabama. He was born in Canton, Mississippi, grew up in La Place, Louisiana, and lived most of his adult life in Texas and California. He now resides on the rim of an ancient meteor impact crater near Wetumpka, Alabama with his wife Theresa and two Afghan Hounds, Niki and Howl.